There was a pause. A pause in which she held her breath, waiting for him to sign off the call, yet hoping he would not. Not yet.

Then he said, "I think this might be the longest time you've gone without asking when I'm coming home."

"When are you coming home?" she asked, her voice deadpan.

His laugh was a deep sexy rumble. And then he hung up.

Nora kept the phone cradled in her hands as if it might help keep the warm fuzzy feelings tucked all around her.

Crushes were nice, she decided. Now, when she thought of Ben—and she thought of him far more often than was in any way sensible—she knew that he was many things. Wry, generous, conflicted, strong-minded, too handsome for his own good, a workaholic. A man who'd dedicated his life to getting people out of trouble. A man, she was beginning to believe, who was rather lonely out there in the big city.

A confidant.

A friend.

But still, it was just a crush...

Dear Reader,

I dedicated this book to a concept that has been bandied about quite a bit these past months: home.

Working from home. Being stuck at home. Forced to stay at home. Unable to go home. Home has loomed large in our lives of late and rarely with a positive spin.

But for me, my home is a sanctuary. It's my happy place. It's my bliss. During these strange times, I have made every effort to keep it that way, steadfastly, deliberately, as my young family and I snuggled in together to see out the storm.

Nora, our heroine, has never really had a home and made it her mission to keep it that way. She won't miss it if she's never had it! Our hero, Bennett, on the other hand, is all but convinced he's made a new home for himself on the other side of the world from where he grew up. It takes a big, beautiful, worn-around-the-edges terrace house in Melbourne to show these two very different, very stubborn, people how wrong they both are.

Wherever you are in the world, snuggle in, as Nora and Ben discover what it means to truly feel at home.

Love,

Ally

The Millionaire's Melbourne Proposal

Ally Blake

Recycling programs
for this product may
not exist in your area.

ISBN-13: 978-1-335-40677-4

The Millionaire's Melbourne Proposal

Copyright © 2021 by Ally Blake

This edition published by arrangement with Harlequin Books S.A.

For questions and comments about the quality of this book,
please contact us at CustomerService@Harlequin.com.

Harlequin Enterprises ULC
22 Adelaide St. West, 40th Floor
Toronto, Ontario M5H 4E3, Canada
www.Harlequin.com

Printed in U.S.A.

Australian author **Ally Blake** loves reading and strong coffee, porch swings and dappled sunshine, beautiful notebooks and soft, dark pencils. Her inquisitive, rambunctious, spectacular children are her exquisite delights. And she adores writing love stories so much she'd write them even if nobody else read them. No wonder, then, having sold over four million copies of her romance novels worldwide, Ally is living her bliss. Find out more about Ally's books at allyblake.com.

Books by Ally Blake

Harlequin Romance

A Fairytale Summer!

Dream Vacation, Surprise Baby

The Royals of Vallemont

Rescuing the Royal Runaway Bride
Amber and the Rogue Prince

Hired by the Mysterious Millionaire
A Week with the Best Man
Crazy About Her Impossible Boss
Brooding Rebel to Baby Daddy

Harlequin KISS

The Rules of Engagement
Faking It to Making It
The Dance Off
Her Hottest Summer Yet

Visit the Author Profile page
at Harlequin.com for more titles.

At its heart this is a story about home—not only the roof beneath which you sleep at night, but the city, the people, the music, the memories, the sensations, the spaces that make you feel safe, and comfortable, and most yourself. So, I dedicate this book to whatever it is out there that makes you feel most at home.

Praise for
Ally Blake

CHAPTER ONE

FACE TILTED TO the bright spring sky, Nora Letterman absorbed her daily dose of Melbourne sunshine as she moseyed her way along the beaten-up Fitzroy footpath.

A tram rattled past, rails screeching, sparks shooting skyward from the wires overhead, drowning out the music playing through Nora's earbuds. She danced out of the way of a smiling couple as they all squeezed between a lamppost and a young girl walking four small fluffy dogs.

As moments went, it was pretty perfect, actually; one of a zillion lovely mental keepsakes she'd tuck away for when she left this little pocket of wonderfulness behind.

Which she would do. Any day now.

The eighteen months she'd spent there were the longest she'd stayed in one place. Ever. And she loved it dearly. But at her core, Nora was footloose and fancy-free. It even said so, in faded, scrawling script on the inside of her right arm, alongside a delicate dandelion, petals breaking away and drifting with the breeze.

"Nora!"

Nora looked back over her shoulder as Christos the fruiterer threw her a mandarin, which she swiped out of the air. Spinning to walk backwards, she put a hand over her heart.

Christos called, "The Tutti Fruiti website is such a hit, Nora. Lots of compliments from customers, which I accept on your behalf. Are you sure I can't pay you in fruit?"

"Not unless the phone company accept payment in kind," Nora called back.

Christos grinned. Then he shot her a salute before turning to flirt with the next customer.

Cheeks full with smiling, Nora meandered on, absorbing the cacophony of sensory delights that made this patch of Fitzroy infamous: incense and coffee, flowers and pre-loved clothes, street art and graffiti, multicultural foods and the lingering scent of smoked herbs that might or might not be legal.

Sure, there was a chain chemist or two along the strip, an American burger behemoth on the corner, but for the most part the shopfronts were generational, mum and dad stores, or young entrepreneurs stepping out into the fray. People having a go. Which was why she'd fitted in so quickly.

The fact that so many of them had readily

snapped up the services of *The Girl Upstairs*—Nora's fledgling online creative business—for a website dust-off, virtual assistance, or a vibrant social-media overhaul was yet another reason her time in this place had been so golden.

Gait loose, mind warm and fuzzy, her time her own, Nora slowed outside Vintage Vamp.

Misty, the elegantly boho business owner who'd refused to hire Nora as she believed the internet would cause the downfall of civilisation, mumbled under her breath as she reworked a clothing rail full of brightly coloured kaftans flapping in a sudden waft of breeze.

"Hey, Misty!" Nora sing-songed.

Misty turned, her eyes lit with genuine fondness, before she remembered herself and frowned. "Thought you'd have left us in your dust by now."

Nora rolled her eyes. "Do you really think I'd go without saying goodbye?"

"Good point, Little Miss Sunshine. Not a chance of that. Now, help me. Do I retire these things?" Misty waved a hand over the colourful kaftans. "Or leave them here, in memory of our Clancy?"

As one, both women blinked, breathed out hard sighs, then looked across the road, to the row of terrace houses on the far corner.

Some facades were overgrown with weeds, paint peeling, fretwork rusting; the tenants mostly students and artists who had gravitated to the area. Other properties had been meticulously renovated till they were worth an utter mint. But Nora's and Misty's gazes were caught on the cream-and-copper-hued terrace house right in the middle.

Neither dilapidated, nor pristine, Thornfield Hall—as it had been lovingly dubbed by its longtime owner—was tidy and appealing. It was also the house in which Nora had been lucky enough to live as the single upstairs tenant for the past year and a half.

Its downstairs sitting room was well known around the area as a safe, warm space for book clubs, widows' groups, and a widows' book club. Always open for a quick coffee, a listening ear, a place to grieve, to vent, to go for laughter and company.

Though it had gone quiet in the days since Clancy Finlayson—eighty-something, raucous, divine, and the owner of Thornfield Hall—had fallen ill. She had passed away before any of them had had the chance to ready themselves for the possibility.

"Any news?" Misty asked. "About the new owner?"

Nora shook her head. "Still no word."

It was all anyone had asked since Clancy had passed.

Knowing Clancy as she had, the house might

have been left to some distant relative, or the local puppy shelter.

While Nora had kept Clancy company during her final days at home, she had no more of a clue than anyone else. She'd focussed, as she always did, on the good not the bad, the happiness not the suffering: reading *Jane Eyre* aloud, telling funny stories she'd picked up in the neighbourhood, playing Clancy's favourite records, and making sure Clancy's hair and nails were *en pointe*.

After Clancy had passed, the lawyers had been frustratingly tight-lipped about it all, citing privacy laws, and Nora didn't know where else to turn.

Which was how she'd found herself in her current state of limbo, ready to move on but unwilling to walk away and leave the beautiful old house untended, abandoned to fate, local squatters or graffiti gangs.

There was also the fact that she'd promised Clancy as much.

In those quiet, final hours, with Nora no longer able to hold back the ache that had been building inside her from the moment Clancy had announced she was sick—her insides crazing faster than she could mentally patch up the damage—in a rare fit of poignancy she'd promised Clancy that she'd take care of her beloved house till the new owner took over.

Clancy might not have been lucid, might not have heard a word, but Nora had been on the receiving end of enough broken promises in her life, a promise *from* her was as good as placing her beating heart in someone's open hands.

So she would stay. Bags packed. Money put aside to cover her interim rent. Ready to hand the house keys to the new owner the moment they showed their face. And only then would she move on, leaving behind nothing but warm feelings and pleasant memories.

After all Clancy had done for her, it was the very least she could do.

Misty cleared her throat and shook herself all over. Pathos was not her natural state of being. "Loved the woman to bits, but I'm never going to move these damn things without her."

Nora dragged her gaze and thoughts back to the rack of floaty, wildly coloured garments now flapping in a growing breeze, the Melbourne weather having turned on a dime as it tended to do.

"May I?" Nora asked, bringing out her phone to take a photo.

Misty waved a *whatever* hand Nora's way.

Nora stood back, found the best angles and took a slew of photos, which she'd edit, filter, tag and post later on her *The Girl Upstairs* pages, which had gathered followers like lint on felt from near the moment she'd set them up as a showcase for her clients. If a half-dozen kaftans weren't snapped up within the day she'd eat her shoes.

Thus distracted, she was too slow to move when Misty grabbed a moss-green kaftan with hot pink embroidery and purple fringing and thrust it up against Nora's person. "You must have it. And when you wear it, you'll think of Clancy."

Beneath the sway of the lurid pattern, Nora's hemp platforms poked out from under her frayed denim flares. If she ever wore such a thing, she'd more likely be thinking she looked like a seventies boudoir lamp.

Nora caught Misty's eye, and the gleam of commerce within, then handed over the twenty bucks anyway. It was Nora's mission in life to leave any place, conversation, and moment brighter than when she entered it and if selling a kaftan made Misty feel a little happier, then so be it.

Kaftan draped over her arm, Nora backed away. "Friday night drinks?"

"If you're still here."

"If I'm still here."

With that, Nora waited for a break in the meandering traffic and jogged across the road.

When she reached the front gate of Clancy's old house, she ambled up the front path; past the Japanese myrtle, to the front patio, its fretwork dripping with jasmine, pale green buds just now starting to show. The elegant facade was a little worn around the edges, but still strong and purposeful, like a royal family who could no longer afford servants, but still wore tiaras to dinner.

Using her key, she jiggled the old lock till it jerked open, then stepped inside.

Dust motes danced in the muted afternoon sunshine pouring through the glass panels in the front door. In the quiet it was easy to imagine Clancy's Chloé perfume on the air, Barry Manilow crooning from the kitchen speaker, the scent of Clancy reheating something Nora had cooked on the beautiful old Aga.

A slice of sadness, of *loss*, whipped across her belly, so sudden, so sharp she let out a sound. Her hand lifted to cover the spot but it took its sweet time to ebb.

This… This was the biggest reason why she had to get the house sorted and move on as soon as possible. As strongly as Nora believed in the deliberate collection of happy moments, she'd made a concerted effort in her adult life not to put herself in situations that might bring on sadness, emotional pain, the sense of missing something, or someone.

Connections, friendships, and traditions felt nice, superficially, but they were so dangerous. They made a person feel as if such things might actually last. Shuffled from foster home to foster home as a kid, promises had been made to Nora, hopes raised, then summarily dashed, again and again.

There was no room for hope, or guilt, or expectations, or regret; not if she wanted a happy life. That lesson had been learned, until it was as indelible as any tattoo. And Nora *really*, *truly*, *deeply* wanted a happy life.

And so she woke up smiling, worked hard, kept little in the way of possessions, was nice to people and expected nothing in return, so that when she moved on, no part of her was left behind. Only a fond lustre, like the kiss of the first cool breeze of autumn at the end of a long summer.

The sudden clackety-clack of toenails on the hardwood floor split the silence, then stilled, snapping Nora back to the present.

"Magpie?" she called, her voice wavering just a smidge. "Pie?"

Pie was a bad-tempered, one-eyed, silky terrier; the latest in a long line of dogs Clancy had fostered in the time Nora had lived there. He'd been due to go back to Playful Paws Puppy Rescue around the time Clancy had passed. But after hearing the news, they'd said it was no rush getting him back.

This wasn't their first rodeo.

So, she was not only stuck looking after a house that wasn't hers, but also a dog that didn't much like her. Which mucked with her head

more than she liked. This had better get sorted…
and soon.

Nora reached slowly into her tote for the baggie of dried meat she'd picked up at the wholefoods market. "I got you a little treat, Pie. Want some?"

She earned a distant growl for her efforts, before the flap of the doggie door gave her reprieve.

Stepping deeper inside the house, her foot caught on the mail that had been slipped through the mail slot in the front door.

A couple of department store mailers, Clancy's subscription to *Men's Health* magazine—for the articles, she'd always claimed—and an official-looking envelope. The latter was thick and yellow, the Melbourne address of a London law firm etched into the top left corner.

And it was addressed to Nora.

Heart kicking till she felt it in her neck and in a flush across her cheeks, Nora moved to the steep stairs leading up to her first-floor apartment, and sat, popping her tote and new kaftan beside her. Then she opened the envelope without ado.

As expected, it was news of Clancy's will, as it pertained to one Nora Letterman.

She knew nothing would be left to her; she'd made Clancy promise after the older woman had made noise about leaving her a sideboard she'd admired. Unless it would fit in her rucksack, it would only be a burden. From what Nora could ascertain from the legalese, Clancy had listened. Apart from a few charitable bequests, the house and everything Clancy owned had been left to one Bennett J Hawthorne.

An answer. Finally!

Though while she felt the expected relief, hot on its heels came a wave of uncomfortable tightness in her belly.

Bennett J Hawthorne. *Bennett*. It had to be Clancy's adopted grandson who, from the little Nora had gleaned, had lived with Clancy from when he was quite young.

Poor guy. What rotten news. And to find out his adoptive grandmother was gone while so far away. Actually, where was he again?

The dozen odd times his name had come up someone had always changed the subject, so she'd never heard the story behind his adoption. Since mere mention of Bennett had always made Clancy maudlin, which was the opposite of Nora spreading sunshine wherever she went, and in her experience "family" was as often considered a dirty word as not, she'd happily let it be. And never thought more of it.

Now she wished she'd pressed. Just a little.

Rubbing a finger and thumb over her temple, she searched her memory banks for the times she'd heard mention of his name.

Once a month or so, Clancy would answer the phone, her face pinched, her shoulders tight, and she'd quietly take the phone to her bedroom. One of those times Nora had heard Clancy say, "Bennett" just before the bedroom door snicked shut.

Was that it?

Then it hit her.

Bennett. *Ben.*

Deep into the night, near the end, perhaps even the very last time Clancy had been in any way lucid, she had muttered, "Ben." Then, louder, more insistent, *"Ben? Is that you?"*

"Ben? Ben who? Would you like me to find him?" Nora had asked, not realising at the time Clancy had meant Bennett, the prodigal, *hush hush* adopted grandson. "Ask him to come?"

"No," Clancy had shot back, her face twisting as if in pain. "Leave him be."

Leave him be. As if asking a guy to take the time to visit his ailing grandmother was too great a burden.

Nora shifted on the stair, the skinny plank of wood with its threadbare patch of old carpet biting into her backside, her initial feelings of *poor guy* having morphed into *what the heck?*

This was the person Clancy had left her beloved Thornfield Hall to? Seriously, what kind of man treated a person that way? Never visiting, calling but rarely. Especially someone as vibrant and loving and wondrous and accepting as Clancy?

Nora allowed herself a rare moment of indulging in feeling all the feelings—the gutting sorrow, the flutters of rage—letting them stew till they coagulated in an ugly ball in her belly before she sucked in a deep soothing breath and reduced them to a simmer.

It took longer than she'd have liked to let it go. But she managed. Letting go of ugly feelings was something she'd long since learned to do with alacrity and grace.

Happiness over suffering.

This was the news she'd been waiting for, unexpected outcome or no. Bennett Hawthorne could come and grab the keys, she'd politely talk him through the vagaries of the old home—the upstairs window that had been painted shut, the noisy downstairs pipe, the wriggly front door lock—then she could draw a nice clean line under what had been a wonderful chapter of her life.

Before the place got its claws into her any deeper. Before this pile of bricks, this street, these people, began to feel like something as insidious and treacherous as *home*.

Nora lifted the papers in her hand, flipped the page and read on, hoping to find a timeline as to when Hawthorne might finally show up so she could be ready.

But then she reached a section that left her a little stunned, as if she'd been smacked in the side of the head.

While the house would go to Bennett Hawthorne, Clancy's will also declared that one Nora Letterman, aka *The Girl Upstairs*, had the right to stay on in the house for a period of up to two months from the date of Clancy's death.

A cleaner would be paid for by the estate. All upkeep and utilities as well. And Nora was not to pay a cent of rent.

The house was not to be open for inspection, put on the market, or in any way renovated during the time Nora was in residence.

She was—of course—welcome to leave sooner if she desired. But the rooms were hers, for two months, if she needed them.

All of which, apparently, suited Bennett Hawthorne, as the reason the letter was from the Melbourne office of a London law firm was because the guy was London-based and thus would not be able to inspect the property in person any time soon.

"Oh, Clancy." Nora breathed out audibly, the letter falling to her knee, her gaze lifting to glance into the kitchen.

The kitchen said nothing in return. Though, in the silence, the clackety-clack of tiny doggy claws echoed somewhere in the big empty house.

Clancy *knew* Nora was a wanderer. They'd often chat about where Nora might end up next; Clancy wistfully sighing over Nora's stories of camping out on other people's sofas, slinging coffees in a train station café for a day in order to be able to afford the fare to get her to the next place, as if that life were something to aspire to rather than a case of needs must.

So what had she been thinking, sneaking this into her will?

Nora felt the slightest twinge tugging on her watch-out-ometer, as if she'd somehow found herself swept up in some larger plan. But she quickly shook it off. Clancy didn't have it in her to be so manipulative. She'd been good, through and through. The best person Nora had ever known. And now she was gone.

"Dammit." Nora rubbed a hand over her eyes, knees juggling with excess energy as she mentally gathered in all the parts of herself that were threatening to fly off into some emotional whirlwind.

Breaking things down into their simplest forms:

Clancy was simply being kind.

But staying was impossible.

So this Bennett guy *had* to come back. Now.

Irresponsible or no, on the other side of the world or not, whatever the story, he was one of Clancy's people. And Clancy never gave up on her people. He'd know what this house meant to his grandmother. And would take care of it.

If not…

While Clancy had loomed large in Nora's life these past months, had treated her with such kindness, respect, and fierce support, she wasn't family. So, it was actually none of Nora's business.

Ignoring the latest twinge *that* brought on, Nora grabbed her phone and searched for Bennett Hawthorne, but she had no clue what he might look like and, since he was adopted, she couldn't even look for a similarity to Clancy. A plethora of images and articles popped up, all the same, most regarding the sweet-looking, elderly mayor of some small town in America who'd tried to make it so that dogs could legally marry one another. Ah, algorithms.

Figuring it mattered little—the guy was who he was—she popped her phone away, grabbed the legal letter, took it upstairs, turned her Taylor Swift playlist up nice and loud, and emailed the lawyers.

CHAPTER TWO

"MR HAWTHORNE?"

Bennett Hawthorne lifted a quieting finger towards the voice at the office door while he listened, hard, to the message left on his phone by the head of his insolvency division…

Dammit.

Word on the street had been that simply by signing with Hawthorne Consultancy, Metropolis Air was set to be released from their involuntary administration order, the firm's brand of zealous forensic accounting and future planning as good as a golden ticket out of bankruptcy.

The street had been misinformed.

Bennett felt the dig of his short blunt fingernails in his palms, and slowly unfurled his fingers.

It was a blow. Time now concertinaed, the team would need to be scrappy and smart to pull this off. But hard work wasn't the problem. He relished the physical and mental satiation that came with hard work; the kinds of days where he fell asleep the moment his head hit the pillow.

It was just that this week, of all weeks, he could have done with an easy win.

If he closed his eyes, he could still hear the exact timbre of the attorney's voice, dry and sober, as she'd sat on the other side of his desk and read from a sheet of paper. "Clancy Finlayson passed peacefully in her sleep a week ago Friday. Cause of death, cancer of the pancreas. Cremation took place three days later. No funeral, by request of the deceased."

A wash of pity had passed over the attorney's face at the last, as she apologised, prodigiously, for the delay in passing on the news, assuring him that the timing had been stipulated, in unflinching detail, in the will.

It had been written that he was *not to be disturbed*.

Disturbed.

They'd had their issues, he and Clancy, but he struggled to accept she'd actually believed that was how news of her passing would affect him.

Then again, *disturbance* could account for his wandering mind, the fitful sleep, the fact he'd listened to the rumours about Metropolis Air and believed them. All reverberations from that initial hit. He only wished he knew when the aftershocks would end.

Bennett pressed finger and thumb into his temples.

No. Likelihood was, he could do with a day

off. To see daylight while outdoors rather than through the floor-to-ceiling windows in his office suite high up in The Shard. To watch something more diverting than the Bloomberg channel.

But with the volatility of the current market, finance was fast, furious, and fragile. Cowboy investors and workaday drones, old apparatuses and new technologies, government turnovers and special interest groups were all scrambling to find their feet in the new order. If he stepped off the treadmill, he'd lose traction and never catch up to where he was today.

Clancy's voice echoed in his head. "Life is change, kid. Making hard choices on the fly is all we can do. It's also short as hell. Don't you dare mourn an old lady who had a good run; worry about your own life."

"Mr Hawthorne—?"

Ben rubbed a hand over his face, tossed his phone onto the couch beside him, and looked to the younger man hovering in the doorway.

Every year Bennett hand-picked a bunch of the first-year employees and put them on an assistant/mentee rotation with the heads of departments. Meaning Damon had been in the room when Clancy's lawyer had dropped her bombshell. The kid was keen, canny and discreet, and Ben couldn't have been more grateful Damon's turn had fallen into this quarter.

"What's up?" Ben asked.

Damon held up a tablet. "You wanted me to let you know when we heard back—"

"I just got word," said Ben with a dismissive shake of his hand.

Damon shook his head. "Not the Metropolis Air hearing. The lawyers. Apparently, there's an issue regarding Nora Letterman."

Ben raised an eyebrow.

"The girl upstairs from your grandmother's—"

"Right," said Ben, cutting him off. The last thing he had time for right now was managing the feelings of one of Clancy's band of merry acolytes.

Damon glanced over his shoulder, towards the bustling workplace outside the door. "I think you need to see it."

Ben waved Damon into the room. The kid was smart. Didn't need the whole office listening in. Work was work. Private life was private. Compartmentalising the two kept things clean. Tidy. Efficient. If numbers were his thing, high drama was definitely not.

Ben stood, buttoned his suit jacket, and moved to sit in his big leather office chair. The desk— with its smoky glass windows and imposing view of London from his corner office—was a better spot from which to make important decisions.

He began, "So, you mentioned an issue."

Damon landed with a lanky *kerflunk* in the

chair on the other side of the desk and tapped the tablet. "Paraphrase?"

"Please."

"Cool. So, she's sorry for your loss. But while Nora is appreciative of Clancy's offer, she'd actually rather not stay."

Ben waited. Realised he'd have to keep on waiting unless he spoke. "That's it?"

"In a nutshell. She also looks forward to you 'coming home', so she can 'hand over the keys in person', which was a promise she made to your grandmother 'on her deathbed'." Damon didn't hold back on the air quotations. "That's pretty much the gist."

Ben sat back in his chair; the absorbers sighing as it rocked him gently in place, his mind no longer wandering.

While the lawyer had winced when reading the subsection of the will regarding the tenant, Ben had been relieved. The existence of a grey-haired, sparkly-eyed, slightly stooped woman keeping watch over the house seventeen-thousand-odd kilometres away gave him breathing space; a good month or two before he had to make any decisions regarding the estate. Before he had to really think about it at all.

Turned out the universe was not about to give him a break this week, at all.

Done with his wandering mind, or any excuses for anything less than his usual mental acuity,

Bennett grabbed a sharpened pencil from the stash kept in his World's Best Boss mug on his desk, opened a fresh notebook to the first page, wrote *The Girl Upstairs* on the title page, and readied to tackle the issue at hand.

"She'd rather not stay," Bennett repeated, jotting down the words, then letting his fingers scribble, sketch, and shade, his mind following.

It seemed odd. Why would Clancy make the offer if it wasn't fait accompli? Was this woman simply being polite? Was she looking for solace? Was she angling for a better deal?

Ben looked down at the page to find a series of zigzags. "The stairs."

Years back, in the before, he'd tried to get Clancy to sell the old terrace house because of the dodgy old staircase. She'd laughed at the very thought. She'd finally agreed to move into the downstairs section, after he'd paid to have a second bathroom put in.

"The stairs?" Damon asked.

"Too small for my feet, even as a kid," he muttered. "They'd be a hazard for old knees. Have the lawyers let Ms Letterman know she's to use the ground-floor rooms only. And look into liability on that score."

Damon blinked, a smile tugging at the corner of his mouth, as he reached over the desk and handed Ben the iPad.

"There's more?" Ben asked.

Damon shook his head. "I don't think *old* knees are the problem."

The tablet was open to an Instagram page.

Ben's gaze skipped over photos of what looked like a row of dresses hanging on a rack, a fruit and veg platter, the shopfront of a florist bursting with arrangements. Glaringly bright, a cacophony of colour, the page was an assault to eyes that were used to the more subtle nuances of a London winter.

"What am I looking at?" Ben asked.

"Nora Letterman."

"Where?" Was she hiding behind a cantaloupe?

"The whole thing. It's her page."

Ben looked up. "She's on *Instagram*?"

Clancy had refused to even have a smartphone, sticking with one of those flip things, a clamshell phone, even though she jumped every time it snapped shut. At least, that was how she'd been a couple of years back, at the time of his last visit. Before everything went to hell.

Damon leant back in the chair, a definite gleam in the eye. "Keep scrolling."

Bennett—who most certainly did not have time for *this*—scrolled with speed through the feed.

More colour-rich photos of café menus, a clutch—compendium? flurry? sneeze?—of orange kittens that made him itch just to look upon them, and street art that was so indicative of the kitsch, anti-establishment mien of Fitzroy he'd have recognised the place even without the slew of energetic hashtags.

For all that they were a violation of the retina, the photographs were quite good. The thematic nature also ticked his liking for symmetry and consistency.

And then his thumb came to a sudden halt, pausing to hover over the screen as his gaze snagged on a picture of an actual person.

A young woman, mid-twenties, tucked up on a chair by a window. Long blonde hair in loose braids tumbled over a soft-looking cardigan, the rest of her swamped by what looked like pyjama pants and fluffy socks. A shaft of sunshine hit the side of her face, lighting up a neat straight nose, a smattering of freckles, and huge blue eyes that smiled over the top of a cup as big as a soup bowl.

The heading beneath the image: *My job is better than your job ;)*

As a whole, the image was cosy and appealing, offering the viewer a glimpse into someplace warm and inviting. Artless. Enviable. Private.

But it was the wallpaper behind her that had the wheels in Bennett's mind spinning with crystalline precision for the first time in days. Dark green, it was, and covered in massive brown moths. The woman in the picture was sitting in Clancy's upstairs bedroom.

The next picture showcased what he could only assume were her knees and a goodly part of her bare tanned thighs, poking out of the bath in the upstairs bedroom—the one with the peacock wallpaper. The water very light on bubbles while she read a paperback covered in wet thumbprints…purchased, apparently, from some local bookstore.

Then an image showed her sitting before a massive cheesy pizza at Brunswick Pizza—the décor hadn't changed in twenty years—elbows on the table, chin propped in her palms. Again those eyes, looking through the camera. Right at him.

He scrolled slowly back to the top of the page, which was entitled *The Girl Upstairs*, leaving him in no doubt that Damon had found his new tenant.

Running a hand over his chin, Bennett breathed out hard. Who was this woman in his grandmother's home?

"So what do you think?" Damon asked.

"I think she is unlikely to struggle with the stairs."

"Not so much."

"Did the lawyers send you this?"

Damon shook his head. "I went looking. First thing I'd have done, if I was in your shoes. First thing I ever do before a job interview. Or a blind date."

Ben shot the kid a look, and Damon sat back, hands lifted in surrender.

Ben wasn't on social media. Not personally. He'd outsourced to a brilliant company to look after that side of things for the business, but did not see a single reason why anyone needed to see a photograph of his dinner, or where he went on holiday—if he ever took holidays. It was akin to forcing people to look at one's vacation slide-show, only now people chose to watch on purpose.

What Bennett did with his life was serious. Consequential. Forensic accounting was about uncovering the raw data, the raw truth, from beneath the tangles and fog of human interference. It was more cathartic than yoga—he knew, he'd tried it.

Social media was the antithesis of what he did. All show and no substance. Hooks and tricks and filters and curation; people showing only the side of themselves they thought people would like. And by the tone of the comments and the eye-popping number of followers, Nora Letterman was clearly good at it.

Which had the hairs tickling at the back of Ben's neck.

He'd last spoken to Clancy a month before. Or, thinking back, it might have been closer to two. That was right. It had been her turn to reach out, and she hadn't. Refusing to chase her up, he'd planned to wait until it was his turn again—the deal they'd put in place after the fallout, and he was a man who lived by his deals—but then… the lawyers had shown up.

For the hundredth time since that morning, he wondered: had Clancy sounded unwell the last time they'd spoken? No. She'd sounded…the same: bolshie, impatient, contrite. Talking ten to the dozen in an effort to cover up any discomfort that might arise between them.

Never once had she mentioned feeling off. Or having a tenant. A girl upstairs.

Why was that? Because she knew he'd have asked why. She'd resisted the idea as long as he'd known her. Was she worried he'd have realised something was wrong?

Or had this person, this girl upstairs, been the one to stop her from telling him? Had she seen in Clancy an elderly woman in need and used it to get free rent? If so, it made sense that she'd be keen to scarper, now a new landlord was on the scene.

"I'm afraid your find has opened up more questions than it answered," Ben lamented.

"What would you like me to do?" Damon asked. "Get back to the lawyers? To Ms Letterman? I could slide into her DMs. Get the lay of the land."

Unlike some who found themselves in a position such as his, Ben *liked* to delegate. The same reason he liked to rotate his assistants. He surrounded himself with self-starters. Go-getters. People who didn't require gentle handling. People like him. It was why his success rate was so high.

But this wasn't business. It was personal.

And, incongruently, the thought of anyone sliding into the DMs of the blue-eyed woman curled up on the chair in the sunshine made him feel strangely uncomfortable.

He shook his head. "Good work, though."

Damon unfolded himself from the chair. "No probs. Wanna keep the tablet? Research purposes."

Ben thought of those big blue eyes, the cosy set-ups, the artlessness he didn't believe for a second, and shook the tablet at Damon. "Ms Letterman is neither a job interview nor a blind date."

"Right." The kid grinned and nabbed the tablet back, tucking it under his arm before lolloping out of the room.

Leaving Ben to ponder his next move.

Get the lawyers to tell Ms Letterman she could move out at her pleasure, then ask Clancy's Melbourne firm to have a rental agency let it out? That would mean strangers living with Clancy's furniture. Her books.

Not ideal. Neither was boarding the place up in order to keep it safe till he could figure out the next right move. Which, if he was at all honest with himself, he'd be happy to put off for a very long time.

While Ben couldn't deny the frisson of concern sparking in the back of his head, keeping the girl upstairs *upstairs* might give him time to figure out her angle, while also holding at bay any necessity as to deciding what to do with the house.

For now.

CHAPTER THREE

Nora lay on her bed, staring at the ceiling, random songs from musicals playing in her ears, when her phone quieted a beat as it pinged with a notification. Nora pushed herself to sitting and slid her thumb across the screen to find a new email from Hawthorne Consultancy.

"Here we go," she said, crossing her legs and dragging her laptop onto her lap. Her legs were jiggling by the time she opened the email.

Dear Ms Letterman

Pursuant to your queries regarding your temporary residence at Thornfield Hall, Fitzroy, Victoria, Mr Hawthorne's responses are as follows:

1. As per the stipulation in Ms Finlayson's will, no rent is owing, so please do not allow any concern on that matter to colour your decision to stay in Thornfield Hall for the allotted time.

2. Please forward any and all copies of invoices regarding upkeep of the house to this

email address so that future accounts are paid from this office forthwith.

3. While Mr Hawthorne is delighted that you'd care to meet in person, he has no immediate plans to return to Australia.

4. No smoking.

5. No pets allowed on the premises.

Regards.

Damon Davidson

pp Bennett J Hawthorne

From the desk of Bennett J Hawthorne, Hawthorne Consultancy

Forensic Accounting, Financial Regulation and Compliance, Insolvency and Restructuring

Nora paused the music she'd kept running in the background, the silence only heightening the fact that her brain had gone into a kind of *pfft-cough-splutter* mode.

Flinging her hands out to the side, she blurted, "What the heck am I meant to do with that?"

When she'd promised Clancy she'd look after the house till she put the keys into the new owner's hands she'd meant it. Her intent had been precise, never imagining that the new owner would fob her off onto some lackey, who'd declared the guy might not bother turning up at all!

And as to no *pets*—did the guy not know his grandmother *at all*? Not that Pie was a *pet* so much as a kind of grumpy, temporary house guest who had not warmed to his host at all.

The point being, this house deserved better. This community deserved better. The memory of the woman who'd helped raise him deserved better.

Nora had only a shadow of a memory of her own father, an artist and musician who'd tried to take care of her after her mother had died, but whose own demons had led him to letting her go. But she feared, now that that memory was mostly an amalgamation of the revolving door of grim-faced foster parents who'd taken her in, found her "too spirited, too needy, too much", and one after another blithely sent her on her way.

She'd have given anything to have a woman like Clancy in her corner. To have that kind of consistency, that support, that love.

Nora's right knee began to jiggle again. A few slow breaths usually calmed that down, but she didn't feel like being calm. She felt offended on Clancy's behalf. That her adopted grandson had grown too selfish or too lazy to take up his family responsibility.

Meaning Nora was caught between the proverbial rock and a hard place: her *mission* to sprinkle sunshine wherever she went, to be helpful without being a nuisance, without pushing too hard, or being "too much", and her *need* to fulfil her promise to Clancy, to repay Clancy for all of her kindnesses so that she could leave this place with not a skerrick of regret.

Both knees now jiggled, and her fingers flicked at the ends of her thumbs, as the solution came to her. Like a big bright light bulb flickering to life overhead.

Clancy's heir might not yet know it, but she was about to help him in a big way.

Nora was going to charm Bennett Hawthorne into coming home.

Once the decision was made a preternatural calm overcame her. She could do this. It would take finesse, and restraint, and careful choices. But she could do this.

First step: make it past the assistant to the man himself.

She reached for a notebook on the bedside table, grabbed a pen, and opened it up to a fresh page. In her neat, blocky handwriting she jotted down the few random things she could remember people saying about him before Clancy had shut them down.

Then she stretched out her fingers, pressed *reply* on the email, and began to type.

Dear Damon
So nice of you to get in touch! Though I was rather hoping to connect with Mr Hawthorne himself.

Despite Clancy's truly gorgeous offer to have me stay in her beautiful home, I am sure Mr Hawthorne is keen to visit the house that has been left to him as soon as possible without some stranger in the way.

The house in which he learned to play "Baby, One More Time" on the trumpet. The rooms Clancy decorated in black wool spiderwebs the year he decided he wanted to be Spiderman when he grew up. The kitchen where he danced to celebrate the first morning he'd not wet the bed. So many warm, wonderful memories.

Rent is not the issue. I'm happy to go with his wishes either way on that score, as he is the new owner of the property. And I will move on without a fuss the moment he arrives and takes the front door key from my hot little hand.

Perhaps you could mention that to him next time he pops his head out from behind his "desk"?

Cheers!

Nora

She added her mobile number, her Instagram handle, along with several other ways in which he could get in touch. Then, after a beat, she deleted her usual *The Girl Upstairs* signature footer and added:

From the desk of Nora Letterman, the Girl Upstairs
Lover of Dandelions, Dragonflies and Rainstorms
on Summer Afternoons.

Sassy, yes. But she could live with that. Before
she could edit, or change her mind, she hit *send*.

Then, feeling full of energy all of a sudden,
she decided to get a head start on the next day's
jobs.

The Ambrosia Café down the street was having a two-for-one coffee promotion that Nora had
agreed to hawk all over their social media pages
and hers, and, unlike some people out there in
the world, Nora did not make a habit of letting
people down.

A dank drizzle had settled over London earlier
that week, creating a permanent oppressive gloom,
but now the rain was coming down so hard, it
pelted against the glass of Ben's office windows
and smudged any effort at a view.

"Mr Hawthorne."

Bennett blinked, and turned away from the
window, to find Damon hovering in the doorway. Again.

"I heard back. From Nora. The girl upst—"

"Yes, I know who she is." Her face had popped
into his mind at the most inconvenient moments

over the past day or so. Likely, he figured, because he was wishing for just a smidge of the shard of sunshine that she'd captured so cleverly. "All settled, I hope."

"Not exactly. She's still determined to leave."

"Seriously?" Dammit. Dammit. *Dammit*. "Is she fishing for something, do you think? A payment? A share?"

Damon blinked, as if it had never occurred to him. "I don't get that feeling. I think she just wants to speak to you. Directly."

"Why?"

"Ah…there was mention of your particular connection to the house. Spiderman decorations, Britney Spears and…other things."

Britney Spears? Bennett reached for his phone as Damon said, "I've forwarded it to your personal email as it felt a smidge, well, personal."

Damon moved *into* the room, after silently shutting the door. It was becoming a habit.

Bennett scrolled through the personal account he rarely used to find emails from a gym he no longer frequented and juice bar newsletters he didn't remember subscribing to till he found the one in question.

And read it.

What the ever-loving—?

"I did *not* wet the bed," he growled.

Damon held up both hands in surrender. "Know

my mum five minutes and she'll tell you I used to eat dirt and wanted to be a turtle when I grew up. We all have a past."

Bennett grunted. "You know way too much about me. I may never be able to let you leave this room."

Damon only grinned. "She's feisty, though, right?"

"I think the term you are looking for is passive aggressive."

"Tom-ay-to, tom-ah-to." A shrug, then, "I like her."

Those big blue eyes swam back into Bennett's consciousness, as well as the strange sensation that she could see to the bottom of his clouded, grey soul. Whatever Damon saw on his boss's face, he lost the grin.

"Okay. So what do we know?"

Bennett refocussed. This was his wheelhouse; he took messy situations, broke them down to their origin, and fixed them.

"She wants out. No one is forcing her to stay. So what's keeping her there?"

"Perhaps," said Damon, "*you* could ask her."

Dealing with a house on the other side of the world was one thing. Dealing with Clancy no longer living in that house required space in his head he simply couldn't commit to right now. Except a spanner in the works, by the name of Nora Letterman, was not going to let it be.

"Just saying," Damon said as he backed out of the office, leaving Bennett to stare at his phone, while running a hand over his mouth as he decided how to approach this.

He took messy situations, broke them down, and fixed them.

The very first question he had every employee ask every client who walked through their door was: who are you, and what do you want? Often times they didn't know themselves until Bennett had found their pressure points and given them a little squeeze.

Ben felt *something* was going on with the woman in Clancy's house, he just couldn't put his finger on it. But the deeper truth was, he didn't want to put his finger on it. Not now. Not yet.

So his next step was to find out who Nora Letterman was and what she wanted.

To: Nora Letterman, The Girl Upstairs
From: Bennett J Hawthorne
Dear Ms Letterman
My assistant Damon passed on your details after your recent correspondence.

Please advise your leave date and I'll call Clancy's lawyers and have them collect any and all keys at your earliest convenience.

Until then, know how deeply I appreciate the fact that someone Clancy trusts so implicitly is taking care of her home until other provisions are made. As you said yourself, Thornfield Hall was very important to her.

If there is anything you require in order to make your stay more comfortable please let me know.

Sincerely

Bennett Hawthorne

To: Bennett Hawthorne

From: Nora

Dear Bennett—or do people call you Ben? Benji? Benny-Boy?

I'm Nora, by the way. Just Nora. "Ms Letterman" sounds like the admin officer at a strict all girls' school.

Pleased to finally "meet" you! Though meeting you in person will no doubt be even better. I have so many stories to share about Clancy's last months: the people she helped, the havoc she caused. Passing those stories on to you will be cathartic—for us both.

If it's concern over the work to be done—finding, sorting, collating and donating Clancy's things—which is hindering your immediate return, please let me know if I can help. It must seem such a daunting task.

If you'd prefer me to leave it all be, then of course that's what I'll do. I can keep to my little cave upstairs, leaving Clancy's private corner of the house just for you.

Other than that, there is nothing I need. Easy-peasy is my middle name.

Thank you for asking.

Cheers,

Nora

PS Apologies for the bed-wetting thing. I'm almost sure I was thinking of someone else.

PPS My middle name is actually Betty. I know. I sound like I ought to be Clancy's grandmother. My dad was a muso and named me after the last two songs he'd heard on a jukebox in the Irish pub in which he was playing the night I was born.

PPS What does the J stand for in Bennett J Hawthorne? John? Jeremiah? Jehoshaphat?

To: Damon Davidson, Hawthorne Consultancy
From: Nora
Damon,
Thanks so much for nudging your boss into connecting. Whatever magic you sprinkled, it worked.
Cheers,
Nora xxx

To: Nora Letterman, The Girl Upstairs
From: Bennett J Hawthorne, Hawthorne Consultancy
Dear Nora
Bennett is fine.

Please do not concern yourself with sorting or collating. It's not an immediate concern. I am in the midst of a deeply complicated case at work and I simply cannot get away.

As to any concerns, are you satisfied with the security measures? It took some convincing for Clancy to allow me to put in the alarm, but I would be happy to organise security cameras as well. Whatever it takes to make you feel comfortable and safe in the interim.

The J stands for Jude.
Regards
Bennett

To: Bennett
From: Nora
Bennett Jude! Not only do we have Clancy in common, we have musical leanings to our names. I'd love to hear the story of how that came about. Something we can save for when you arrive to take over the house, perhaps.

There's an alarm? Huh… I had no clue. BRB.

Yep. Found it! Behind a plant in the front hall. Any clue what the code is? Probs best if I don't guess. Might bring a fleet of those little hatch-backs to the door. Firefighters, on the other hand… ;)

Actually, don't worry about the code. If I've been fine till now I'll be safe enough during the short time I'm here before you make it back. Anyway, the back door doesn't exactly lock right; I nudge a chair against the handle at night. That plus a copy of *Wolf Hall* on top. At six-hundred-odd pages the thing is overwhelming, but as door wedges go, it's the perfect fit.

Are you a reader like Clancy? If not I'll make sure to pop it back on the shelves before you come. The thing is seriously intimidating.

Cheers,

Nora

To: Nora

From: Bennett

Nora,

Please pass details of the security company to my assistant, Damon, so that a new password can be organised.

At six foot five inches, feeling intimidated by size is not a concern of mine.

Jude was Clancy's father's name.

Regards

Bennett

To: Bennett
From: Nora

Six foot five? Yikes! How on earth did you ever navigate Clancy's stairs? I have to take care not to trip up the things every day and I have unusually dainty feet.

As for the alarm—I've always slept with a stump of wood under the bed. If anyone does break in, they're in for a rude shock. So don't bother Damon with it. I'm sure he's busy enough, getting your extra-long suits dry-cleaned and bringing you hot, black, single-blend coffees all day long.

I have clearly picked up my vision of what an assistant does from Nancy Meyers movies!

Unless you're really as swamped at work as you intimated, meaning you probs don't have time for entertainment-type things. Just in case, movies are like newsreels, only made up, books are words on pages all bound together that hit you in the face as you fall asleep reading, and music is the thing your phone's ringtone is based on.

You're welcome.

N

PS What on earth is Forensic Accounting, Financial Regulation and Compliance, Insolvency and Restructuring in plain English?

To: Nora
From: Bennett
Nora,
I would feel better knowing the house is fully secure, lump of wood under the bed aside. Next time Damon brings me a coffee—cream, three sugars—I'll ask him to get in touch.

As to my work: I take struggling companies, figure out where they went wrong by following the numbers, help them create new business practices, and restructure them so that they might live to see another day.
Take care on the stairs. Please.
Bennett

To: Nora
From: Damon
Nora, hey!
Mr Hawthorne has asked that I grab the details of the security company in charge of your alarm. If you could send me the deets, that'd be great.

And I'm also to remind you to please take care on the stairs.
Damon

To: Damon
From: Nora
Aw... Both of you reminding me to take care on

the stairs makes me feel so…so certain you are unsure of your liability if I'm hurt.

I hereby release the Boss Man of any blame if I'm a goof on the Thornfield Hall stairs. That do? Great.

As to the other thing… I'm all good.

Cheers!

N

PS Does your boss really take three sugars in his coffee?

To: Bennett
From: Nora
You help companies so that they "might live to see another day"?

That's impressive.

Might I even suggest…heroic?

N

To: Nora
From: Bennett
It's satisfying work, yes. But I can attest to the fact that I have never—not once—walked around at work feeling particularly heroic.

B

To: Bennett
From: Nora
Have you tried wearing a cape?

To: Nora
From: Bennett
Do you know how hard it is to find a cape to match your tie?

To: Bennett
From: Nora
Ha! Yeah, I can see how that might be a problem. Something you can get Damon onto, perhaps? Give him something to do other than buff his nails and flirt with the other assistants. Just spit-balling here...

In case you're wondering, but are just too polite to ask, I also have my own business. *The Girl Upstairs*. I manage social media pages, build manageable websites, act as virtual assistant to work-from-homers—that kind of thing.

I might not wear a cape, but I feel I make a difference. That I am of use. Which is a really nice thing.

Actually...do you ever do what you do for smaller companies? On the quiet, there are a couple of local businesses who I'm sure could do with a sprinkle of your expertise. Ones who need more than a new website and shareable self-promotion to stay afloat.

Maybe when you come—you know, to grab the keys and take over the house—I can nudge a few of them your way? Yes? Really? Excellent!

From your partner in spreading goodness all over the world,
Nora

To: Bennett
From: Nora
Hey, all okay?

To: Bennett
From: Nora
Hope I didn't offend you with my assumption that you need an assistant to buy your capes, when, in fact, you are world-famous for your cape-buying abilities.
N

To: Bennett
From: Nora
Hi! Remember me?
I know you're busy saving the world, one corporation at a time, but if you could assure me you didn't manage to find a cape to match your tie only for it to get caught in the engine of your private jet and strangle you, that'd be great!

Unless…gasp! Are you currently en route? About to arrive at my—aka your—front door with a flourish?

See, I now can't imagine you without a cape! Not that I've imagined you…

Yours
Nora

To: Nora
From: Bennett
Dear Ms Letterman
Apologies for my lack of response. Things have rather blown up at work.

I humbly request we put our correspondence on the back burner—at least until I am able to put the current situation to bed.

I continue to appreciate your taking care of Thornfield Hall.

In the meantime,
Sincerely
Bennett Hawthorne

Ms Letterman?

Nora reeled away from the laptop with such speed she nearly hit her head on the headboard.

Really? They were back there again? After a week of emails back and forth, of her bag remaining unpacked, future plans unplanned? She'd been certain she'd made headway; softening the guy up, getting Damon on side, giving him a dozen reasons to come home.

Now she had the awful, cheek-warming, neck-tingling, stomach-dropping feeling he'd been stringing her along, knowing he had all the power and could cut her loose without a word.

Dammit. Damn all six feet five inches of him— if Bennett J Hawthorne was *really* that tall. Guy was probably shorter than her. And compensating.

Without taking a single extra moment to think, Nora pressed *reply*.

To: Bennett
From: Nora. Just Nora
Dear Mr Hawthorne
I'm afraid "putting our correspondence on the back burner" does not work for me. In the meantime or any time.

In case I've been too subtle, or you are immune to my clever ploys, or you're a tougher customer than I had thought, here goes: COME HOME AND TAKE CARE OF YOUR GRANDMOTHER'S HOUSE.

Appreciate my presence here all you like, but I am only here for Clancy. I promised her I'd look after the place till the new owner came, and I take promises and responsibilities seriously.

I'd appreciate it if you'd stop taking advantage of my good nature and come home.

If, in fact, you know all this, deep down beneath your big and tall suits, perhaps the fact you do not feel heroic isn't down to your lack of a cape.

The ball's in your court.

Nora

CHAPTER FOUR

Nora sat on a barstool at Shenanigans, nursing a warming gin and tonic and fiddling half-heartedly with filters for an Instagram post about the bar, while the Friday night crowd laughed and danced and flirted and hustled at her back.

Her gin was warm, and her mind wouldn't settle, for it had been three days since she'd last heard from the disappointing Bennett Hawthorne with his "humble requests" and his "appreciation". Three days since her inglorious "the ball's in your court" email.

So much for charming Bennett Hawthorne into coming home.

She'd started out so well—delightful with a hint of optimistic coercion; it was her MO, after all. But she'd soon found herself swept up in his rhythm: wry, dry and a little sly. Used, as she was, to writing upbeat, engaging, client-centric verbiage, engaging in a little light snark had been a kind of relief.

High on sass, she'd taken a misstep somewhere. Only when he'd stopped responding did it hit her that she'd pushed too much, or tried too hard. The realisation had tipped her usually well-restrained sensitivity into umbrage and she'd gone off half-cocked, screwing up all the lovely headway she'd been making.

For all that she favoured being footloose and fancy-free, she wasn't just one thing. Her spectrum ranged from Sunshine Mode Nora to Survival Mode Nora. She'd been at the sunshine end for so long, she'd forgotten how intimately entwined both ends actually were.

Of course, there was the very good chance that while she'd been plying him with her greatest hits, he'd seen her coming from a mile off and played her like a violin.

"Nora the Explorer," said Misty as she appeared at Nora's elbow. "Drinking alone?"

"Just getting a head start," Nora said with a smile. "What'll you have?"

"The same," said Misty, waggling a hand at Sam, the young bartender she had her eye on. He smartly kept his distance, nodding his response. "Was half hoping, for your sake, the wind might have finally swept you off to more exciting climes, like a ladybug on the breeze—"

"A dandelion on the wind." Nora turned over her wrist to show the scattered dandelion tattoo thereupon. "Let's just say, my plan isn't coming together quite as I'd hoped."

"How so?"

"I found out what's happening with Clancy's place. She left it to her grandson."

"You mean *Bennett*?" Misty asked, eyes near popping out of her head.

"That's the one. What was the story there?"

"I didn't live around these parts at the time but apparently Clancy adopted him when he was, like, five. She always called him her grandson rather than her son as she was already in her fifties at the time."

"Well, that's nice." To five-year-old Nora it would have been the dream. And eight-year-old Nora, and thirteen-year-old Nora… "He's her only family, right? So why didn't everyone assume she'd leave the house to him?"

"The Great Falling Out, of course."

A dark little corner of Nora's usually determinedly chipper psyche unfurled itself. "Falling out, you say?" It would explain the shushing.

"Clancy never said anything?" Misty intoned.

Nora shook her head. "Do you know what it was about?" Translation: what on earth did the guy do to upset Clancy so badly? It must have been huge as Clancy was the queen of second chances. And third. She was basically unoffendable.

"We all knew *when* it happened. Bennett was

the light of her life, then, boom, he stopped visiting and a chill seemed to come over the room anytime anyone brought him up. But she refused to give up why."

Nora turned on her seat, warming up to this new development. Anything that might make her feel better about her bad feeling about the guy could only help. "Did you ever meet him?"

"Sure. Plenty."

"What's he like? Cold-blooded? Shark-eyed? Slovenly? A diminutive sociopathic troll?"

Misty blinked. "You've searched him on the internet, right? That's what you young ones do nowadays."

Nora's mouth twisted. "Half-heartedly, back at the beginning. With no luck. Why?"

"First tell me why you're so interested in him."

Misty's gaze turned predatory as she turned to face Nora on her stool. If Nora weren't so stuck on the subject, she'd have changed it. Fast.

"Well…we've been emailing." *Had* been emailing. Past tense.

"Really? *Sexy* emails?"

"What? No! Jeez."

But they had been playful. At first. Sarcasm, irony, verbal acerbity—they were her secret catnip. She'd found herself reaching for her phone the moment she woke up in the morning, in case there'd been a new email overnight. It was how

he'd lulled her into a false sense of security before ghosting her.

"They were…frustrating."

Misty's eyebrows waggled. "Sounds sexy to
me."

"We emailed about his *grandmother*." Nora's voice dropped to a respectful whisper as
she lifted her eyebrows and added, "His *dead
grandmother*. I… I kind of promised Clancy that
I'd look after the house till the new owner came.
And Mr Stuffy McBusiness Suit is taking that to
mean he can go on ignoring his responsibilities!"

"Wow," said Misty, blinking Nora's way. "I'm
not sure I've ever seen you this worked up. You're
always so chilled I had floated the idea you had
some kind of dopamine imbalance."

Nora rolled her eyes, then glanced around to
make sure no one was listening in. "Look, being
'chilled' doesn't exactly come naturally to me.
The bastion of sunshine you see before you has
been diligently cultivated. Over many years."

After the third foster home that had sent her
back for being too loud, too noisy, too demand-
ing, too much, she'd taught herself to pull back,
to be helpful, a force for good, while not taking
up too much space, and leaving nothing of herself behind.

"Being 'chilled'," she admitted, "is hard work."

"Oh, honey," said Misty, on a rare kick of empathy. Then added, "I *like* this side of you. Sassy, sharp, a little groundswell of rage."

"Thanks?" Nora laughed, then rewarded herself with a goodly sip of warm gin.

"Now, you know helping people isn't my thing, but, in the spirit of trying new personalities on for size, I'll give it a go this once."

With that, Misty dragged Nora's phone towards her, and slowly typed letters into a search engine. Unlike Nora had, however, she typed in *Hawthorne Consultancy*.

Clicking the *About Us* page, they found pictures of accountants, and lawyers, and financial advisors. The images were effortless, elegantly casual: people laughing over coffee, or twirling a stylus, or working hard at a laptop.

For a company that sounded as dry as burnt toast, the site had a modern, holistic *trust us, we've got you* vibe. Despite herself, Nora loved it.

"Wait for it," Misty murmured beside her as she continued to scroll through the images—

Whoa, Nelly.

Right at the very bottom of the page, almost an afterthought, was the largest image of all. Beneath the picture it said *Bennett J Hawthorne, Founder of Hawthorne Consultancy*.

Peripherally, Nora noted the Millennium Wheel, an out-of-focus smudge over one shoulder, and the sun glinting creamy gold off the Thames. But her eye was stuck on the man.

Acres of broad-shouldered wonder filled the frame, hard angles wrapped up in a dark suit and a snow-white shirt. His hair was a tumble of thick, chocolatey waves. Strong jaw, freshly shaven, but with a look that said the stubble wouldn't be kept back for long. Intelligent dark eyes looking just off camera.

Thank goodness. Because she wasn't quite sure what she might have done had they been looking at her.

"Not so much a diminutive shark-eyed troll, then."

"Mountainous, in fact. With the eyes of a matinee idol. Pity he's so frustrating."

"Right," Nora murmured. "Pity." Then, "Do you think he's looked *me* up?"

"Ooh. Good point. Did he flirt in your not-sexy emails? Even a tiny little bit?"

Nora thought back to the cape-and-tie comment, the sense that he'd been laughing *with* her. "There were moments where he wasn't entirely exasperating."

"Then he's looked you up for sure. Ooh, I love this song!" With that Misty leapt off the barstool and carved a path to a space in front of the juke-box and began to dance while Nora found herself very glad she hadn't searched deeper before she'd sent her spate of emails. Knowing this was the man she'd been flirting with—not flirting, cajoling—she might well have sent nothing but drool.

Thumb moving slowly, surreptitiously, she clicked back to her search page and under *Images* typed *Bennett Hawthorne Consultancy London*. She found pictures of him at some international symposium, his expression stormy, his shirtsleeves rolled at his elbows, sporting longer hair and a beard—oh, my. There was another with Bennett in a group shot at some charity fundraiser at the Royal Albert Hall, where he stood a half-head taller than everyone else. This time those eyes of his looked directly down the barrel of the lens; darkly intelligent, and stunning.

Mouth suddenly dry, yet somehow also watering, her skin clammy, yet overly warm, Nora put her hand over the screen.

So what if he was gorgeous? It didn't negate the fact that Clancy had fallen ill, had died, had been buried, and he hadn't been there. While Nora would literally have given a kidney to have been adopted into a family, *any* family, much less one of Clancy's calibre, if she'd been given half a chance.

And, despite her setback, she still had a promise to fulfil.

Maybe the problem was the medium. Perhaps her sunshine had got lost in translation over the great distance between them.

If she were to get through to the man, to encourage him home, and at the same time show him what he'd missed by not being there for Clancy, it would be worth it.

It would take subtlety. Savvy. Self-will. And, as Misty had pointed out, if she had to tap, ever so slightly, into the parts of herself she'd spent years holding back—the sass, the spirit, the stubborn refusal to believe no was even possible— then so be it.

An hour later she was home, a little tipsy, but determined.

She opened her laptop, took a deep breath, and typed.

To: Bennett
From: Nora
Ben
Remember me? Nora the delightful?

Now, I know I said the ball was in your court— clearly it always was, and I was just being cute suggesting otherwise—but here I am again. With a tap dance and an apology.

The fact that I haven't heard back from you makes me think that, despite the fact we do not know one another at all, you noticed that I kind of lost my cool.

My reasons, though, were entirely altruistic.

For I believe, deep down inside, that wherever she is Clancy's heart would be breaking at the thought of seeing this place empty. Abandoned. Left to dust.

And I promised—literally promised—I wouldn't let that happen.

I have wondered, since we began to chat, if she knew you wouldn't come running. Perhaps that's even why she put the provision in her will that I stay.

Maybe she wanted me on your case, hoping I'd be able to out-stubborn you, and convince you to come home.

I don't know what happened between the two of you, she never said, but perhaps all of this is her effort at giving you closure, whatever that might mean for you.

Perhaps she wanted you to come home to say goodbye.

Nora

The massive streak of coarse grey fur huffed and puffed and pulled so hard on the lead, Nora could no longer feel her fingers.

"Anyone would think you've never walked a dog before," called Misty as the huge dog dragged Nora past the Vintage Vamp.

"I haven't!" Nora managed, waving as she passed, before using both hands to grip the lead.

None of the families she'd been sent to live with had been the warm and fuzzy types. Which should have told her all she needed to know before she'd let herself get her hopes up about any of them falling in love with *her*. Benefit of hindsight.

She'd visited Playful Paws Puppy Rescue to talk to them about coming to pick up Pie, and somehow been roped into fostering yet another dog, claiming Cutie—that was his name—might draw Pie out of hiding. She should be taking lessons on making people do her bidding from them.

The fact that Mr Stuffy McShoulders had said "no pets" might have been a slight sweetener. Especially since she'd woken to still no response after her *very* nice email overnight.

The breath oofed out of her as Cutie took off across the street. She managed to angle him towards the front gate, up the path and through the front door once she'd managed to jiggle the key in the lock.

Her phone rang just as Cutie bolted, bumping into the walls, sniffing everything, lead following behind him like a manic snake. She could only hope Pie's hiding spot was a good one.

She grabbed her phone, slid her thumb over the answer button, and sing-songed, "The Girl Upstairs!"

The pause was so long, it had to be a telemarketer. She nearly hung up.

Until a voice—deep, rough and definitely male—eventually intoned, "Ms Letterman?"

There was no way she could be certain the voice belonged to who she thought it belonged to. All he'd said was her name, and yet…the way it was said—low, rumbling, with a burr at the edge. *Whoa*. The hairs stood up on the back of her neck. And every cell in her body slowed to a grinding halt.

"That's me," said Nora, her voice a little tight, breathy. "I'm Nora Letterman."

"Bennett Hawthorne."

Her breath left her lungs in a whoosh.

It was him. On the phone. Which was excellent! Her conciliatory little email must have made a difference. Yay her!

Only she wasn't ready for him. Not in the least.

If she'd known he was going to call, she'd have prepared. Done some deep breathing. Plastered a smile on her face then drowned him in kindness till he agreed that she was right and he was wrong.

"Ms Letterman?" That *voice*. It was like molten chocolate. Like promises made in the dark.

"Yes," she croaked. *Water*. Most ailments could be solved by a drink of water. She hustled into the kitchen. Filled a glass an inch and skulled it. "Sorry. Hello! Well, this is unexpected."

"Quite," he responded.

She tapped the phone onto speaker and poured herself another drink. "I'm glad, though. Glad you called. There's a lot to discuss. Unless you're calling to tell me what time to pick you up from Melbourne airport?"

"Ah, no."

"Sigh. Then what can I do for you this fine afternoon?"

Another beat slunk by. "Fine, is it?"

"Mmm-hmm. Sunny, blue skies. Prefect spring day here in Melbourne. You?"

"Cold. Dark."

"Dark? It has to be, what, eight in the morning over there?"

"Seven. And it's raining hard enough I can't see anything beyond my office window."

"Man, you need a holiday. And I know just the place."

Hang on, was that a *laugh*? And had she just called him "man"? Whatever had just happened, he found it necessary to clear his throat before saying, "I am calling to apologise."

"Oh." Oh, indeed. She hadn't expected a phone call, or a chat about the weather. But the number one thing she'd not have expected from this man was an apology.

He went on. "I seem to have said something to upset you in our original email exchange, which was never my intention."

That stopped her with a glass halfway to her lips. "You *seem* to have? According to whom?"

She heard his hesitation. Got the feeling that

for Bennett J Hawthorne it was a highly unusual occurrence.

"My assistant, Damon, pointed it out."

Nora cocked a hip against the kitchen bench and said, "I knew I liked Damon. Right from the outset."

"Mmm," he intoned, his promises-in-the-dark voice dropped, deepened, which she would not have thought possible. "Then you'll be happy to know he's quite taken with you too."

"Not surprising. I am actually very likeable once you get to know me. You can tell him I'm taken with him too."

After that came a stretch of silence. Not thin and chilly, the way it had felt after his last email. Loaded. Weighty. Filled with waiting.

He's stubborn, her subconscious piped up in a panic. *Clever. Disloyal. His interests do not align with yours and you are being super-shallow. You would not be acting this way if you hadn't seen his picture.*

Before she could fully convince herself, the guy had to go and say, "What if I told you Damon had no skills in coordinating ties and capes?"

Nora felt a definite something flicker inside her; the surety the man was flirting. Yes, she'd seen his picture. But they'd toyed with one another, just a little, before she'd had a single clue what he looked like.

She swallowed. "I'd feel shocked. Bemused. Totally off my game."

"Well, we don't want that, now, do we?"

Nora's mouth opened and closed again. She felt as if she'd stumbled into some kind of alternate universe. One in which their emails had gone down a very different path. One in which she and Bennett J Hawthorne were on very different terms.

One in which he wasn't simply a person who she was certain had wronged one of the few people she had ever loved. He was also a person who'd recently lost his grandmother and was struggling to know quite how to deal with it.

Nora gently cleared the tickles from her throat. "Did I imagine it, or did you mention something about an apology…?"

"I did." A beat, a collecting of thoughts, a shift of tone that she could all but hear, then, "Hence the phone call. Text can easily be misconstrued. In my work, subtlety and nuance often breed misinformation and misunderstanding. So, I'm afraid my correspondence tone has, over time, become rather blunt. Which I acknowledge is not conducive to civil conversation outside the business realm."

"I see," said Nora as she tried to navigate the meander back into corporate speak. His comfort zone, she figured. "And?"

"And?"

"And *I'm sorry, Nora*?"

Oh, yeah. That was a definite laugh. Gentle, rough, but there. She felt it skitter down her spine, and land in the backs of her knees.

"And I'm sorry, Nora," he said, his voice quieter now too. More intimate. As if he was trying not to be overheard. As if his words were not for anyone else but her.

Nora held the water glass to her cheek, which seemed to have come over a little warm. "Do you call all the girls you offend over email? Or should I feel special?"

She squeezed her eyes shut; hoping he might not pick up on her own flirty tone if she couldn't see herself doing it.

This time the chuckle was louder. She heard what sounded like the squeak of an office chair. She imagined him leaning back, cocking a foot over the other knee. Running a finger along his full bottom lip—

"Special," he intoned. "Most definitely special."

Nora might have been in danger of losing *all* feeling in the backs of her knees, except a thump from down the hall had her spinning to watch out for a blur of grey fur.

Cutie. Cutie was out there somewhere. As was Pie. Neither of whom she was allowed to have, according to her new landlord. Who was on the phone right now. Her landlord who had responsibilities here. Which he was shirking. To her detriment!

But still…

This *was* progress.

"I hope you accept my apology too."

"For?"

"Calling you out. I may have been a little touchy. This whole thing has been rough. Clancy's passing, waiting to find out what would happen with the house… Taking it out on you was indefensible. And very much not like me."

Again with the pause. As if the man was deliberate in his choice of words. As if nothing he ever said was said by accident.

Nora closed her eyes again, this time against the fact she kept revealing herself to this man. First via email, gushing about how much she loved her job, how helping people made her feel good about herself. Now this…this vulnerability. Talk about not like her!

"So-o-o?" he said, drawing the word out in that cavernously deep voice of his.

"So?"

"I'm sorry, Bennett?"

Nora felt a smile start deep in her belly before it moved, warm and slow, like molten treacle, up her throat and into her cheeks. "I'm sorry, Bennett."

At that the man made a sound in the back of his throat. A deep, rough hum that had her leaning over her phone so as to catch it. Subtlety, nuance and all.

Her feelings just a little raw, and exposed, she found herself saying, "I'm sorry about Clancy too. For your loss. She was a wonderful woman. Possibly the best I've ever known. It must be hard, being so far away, at a time like this."

When her words brooked no response, she quickly added, "That wasn't a tactical manoeuvre, I promise. I meant it."

When she heard a distinct *woof* echo from deep inside the house, she pulled herself upright, grabbed her phone, took it off speaker and jammed it against her ear. "Look, I have to go. But thank you. For the call. And the apology. And keeping the lines of communication open."

"My pleasure."

"But don't think you got off that easily."

Laughter. Absolutely no doubt that time. The kind that sent golden sparks down the back of her neck, which met the warmth in her cheeks and the erratic *ske-bump* of her heart until she felt utterly discombobulated.

"And why's that?" he asked.

Woof-woof. Deep and wall-shaking that time. Definitely Cutie. She only hoped he was standing still. Either that or she'd be spending every cent of her savings on new furniture and hoping Ben didn't notice the difference.

"Because, Ben Hawthorne, one way or the other I'm convincing you to come home."

With that she hung up.

She'd unpack the conversation—the chuckles, and the warm, deep voice, and the complete lack of stuffiness, and her reaction to it—later. Or maybe she wouldn't. Actually softening towards Ben Hawthorne was not an option. Not while there were so many reasons to be disillusioned with the guy.

Pretending she had, on the other hand, might be something she could learn to do.

First, she had to track down the critters who were now running amok in her house.

But it wasn't her house.

It was his.

CHAPTER FIVE

BEN STARED INTO the takeaway container filled with some kind of meatless rice dish Damon had brought in, insisting the "slow-release energy" and "superfood content" was a necessity for "a man with his workload".

As if a week of blocked avenues, stalled agreements, and lack of progress on his current deal was any different from every other client in the same kind of deep mess as Metropolis Airlines.

As if, for some reason, this one was taking a toll.

Scoffing at the very thought, Ben tossed the dish to his desk and picked up his phone. To check his emails. And…other things.

The phone just happened to be open to Instagram. Damon had set him up and bade him follow a few sites—local news, NASA, Celeste Barber. *The Girl Upstairs*.

He'd been aware from the very first email what she was trying to do. She had the subtlety of a velvet-covered sledgehammer. What he should have done was made himself clear, from the out-set: he wasn't coming. Not any time in the fore-seeable future. His life was here. His work was here. That place—the memory of the last time he'd seen Clancy—was something he wasn't pre-pared to relive.

But he'd found himself looking forward to the ping of his phone, in case it heralded another message from her.

Ben sat back in his chair, his thumb swiping slowly down Nora's page. Past a picture inside a bar, everyone out of focus aside from one dancer in the middle, hair flying. Another of a group of women laughing and clinking champagne glasses while painting matching cacti in some kind of class.

His thumb hovered over the screen, no lon-ger scrolling when she appeared on the feed. Hair down, decked out in a long green dress that clipped behind her neck and left her lean, golden-brown arms bare, she leant against a tall menu board, drinking some kind of fruity drink from a huge plastic cup. A dimple popped in one cheek, her face lit with half a smile.

New pictures, all. He knew. It wasn't the first time he'd given up a few minutes of his day in that space.

At first he'd gone back to her page to get a fix of the old area. A place he didn't know he'd been missing. It helped a little, dealing with the fact that he hadn't been there; not just at the end, but for a really long time.

But soon he'd found himself lost in the bright chaotic colour of *The Girl Upstairs* feed, and it felt like sorbet for his brain. There was a vitality to her page—her words, the way she cut to the quick—that he found crisp, bracing, refreshing. A relief from the standard long days and bitterly cold nights.

Ben's phone buzzed and he actually flinched. As if he'd been caught doing something untoward.

He checked the screen to find a video-chatting app flashing a notification at him. Some other thing Damon had no doubt installed in a fit of enthusiasm. The caller was someone by the name of Dandelion.

Ready to put it down to spam, a little twitch in the back of his head made him pause, before tapping the answer button.

Big heart-shaped glasses covered half a woman's face, sunny blonde waves tumbled over her shoulders, lips the reddest red there ever was sucked on a paper straw above a milkshake three times the size of her hand.

Nora Letterman; as if he'd conjured her out of thin air.

"Nora," he said, his voice rough.

"Why hello!" she sang, tipping her glasses slightly forward with a single finger sporting chipped orange nail polish. "If it isn't Bennett Jude Hawthorne himself. I figured I had about a twenty-three per cent chance you'd answer. Even then I was pretty sure I'd be looking at the delightful Damon. But there you are!"

Those big blue eyes of hers, half hidden behind the sunglasses, told a story all their own.

There was an unhurried quality to her, ethereal even, the kind that had made him wonder if the woman he'd imagined he'd been talking to was a figment, a construct. But the easy sway of her shoulders, the gentle clamp of her teeth on the straw, the glint in the small part of her big blue eyes that he could see—she was so real her life force near leapt off the screen.

A wave of attraction sluiced over him, like the water of an outdoor shower on a summer day. It unmanned him. And woke him up.

What was he doing stalking this woman's Instagram, calling her to apologise, just so he had an excuse to keep the conversation going? All he knew about her was that she'd somehow ingratiated herself with Clancy in the final months of her life, and was now trying to do the same to him.

He didn't have Clancy's Pollyanna positivity, he never had—from the moment his mother had left him, he'd been wary, untrusting, and it had served him well—and he didn't know her from Adam. He honestly did not have time for any of this. Or the head space. It was time to demand all future correspondence remain between their respective lawyers.

Instead he found his mouth forming the words, "Twenty-three per cent seems a little high."

She laughed—a light, happy bark—as her head tipped back and her mouth stretched wider than a human mouth ought to stretch. Her phone wobbled as she shifted position. She sat cross-legged on some kind of bench with enough light and colour flashing all around her it looked as if she might be in an arcade.

Then she put down the drink beside her and pulled the glasses right to the end of her nose.

His determination to put an end to their correspondence was no match for the riot of sensation that stampeded through him as he got a load of those eyes. Damn, they were something. Dusky, blue, and tilted in a way that made her look permanently amused.

Nora Letterman had the sort of eyes that made sailors dash themselves against rocky shores. And gladly.

Ben cleared his throat. "What can I do for you, Ms Letterman?"

"Oh, no, we're not going back there again. Not after our heartfelt apologies the other day." Her hand went to her heart, the move tipping the thin strap of her floaty top just off her shoulder. "I'm Nora. And you're Ben. And that's that. Un-

less you think we're up to the nickname stage...
B-Boy. Benny and the Jets. Franklin as in Ben-
jamin."

Ben blinked.

"No? Fine. Ben and Nora, it is." The phone
swung sideways. Lights and music buzzed and
blinged all around her head. Then she lifted a
handful of popcorn and tossed it piece by piece
into her mouth.

Ben found himself leaning in. "Where on earth
are you?"

"I'm glad you asked. I am having dinner at the
night market down the road from your place. It's
new since you were last here. Super swanky."
She took off her glasses and tossed them into a
net bag at her side. "Wanna see?"

Before he had the chance to answer, she
switched the phone away from selfie mode and
gave him a virtual three-hundred-and-sixty-
degree tour of what looked like a 7-Eleven store
mixed with an arcade mixed with a cinema candy
bar. Swanky? It gave him a sugar headache.

Rubbing his temple, he called, "Nora." Then
louder. "Nora!"

It switched back to selfie mode. And once
again he found himself struck, as if he'd been
hit in the back of the head. Those eyes. That
inner light. That smile.

"Cool, huh?" she asked, before her lips once
again puckered around a straw.

"That's your dinner?" he asked, unable to keep focus. "Popcorn and a shake."

A grin. A shrug. "Veggies and dairy. Boom." She turned her head, beamed at someone passing by. "Hey, Ross."

"Hey, Nora," said a deep male voice before a face popped into view, bussing a kiss to her cheek.

"Ross," she said, jabbing a thumb at thin air once the man had moved on. "Owns the local florist. One of the businesses I'd mentioned to you who could really do with your professional heroic eye."

Ben ran a hand up the back of his neck, gripping it tight, and tried not to wonder what else Ross might mean to Nora. It was none of his business. *She* was none of his business. In fact, she was a thorn in his side, a pain in his neck, and a dangerously disruptive influence in his heretofore tightly engineered life.

All of which she managed from the other side of the planet.

Imagine what havoc she might cause if he actually went home—

Not home. Melbourne. Home was London and had been for a number of years. In fact, he'd likely spent more hours in this office than he had in Thornfield Hall. He was exactly where he was meant to be.

"Why are you calling, Nora? Is there an issue with the house?" he asked.

He could have sworn her left eyelid flickered, before she said, "Nope! Everything's perfect."

"Then what can I do for you?"

Her hair bounced as if she was now kicking the wall of the counter on which she sat. "Do I really need to say it?"

Ben knew what she wanted. She wanted him to get on a plane, grab a cab to Fitzroy, and take the keys from her hand. He shook his head.

"Okay, then. So what do you think of the night market, huh?"

"It's giving me a tension headache."

She laughed, and it made her face even lovelier than it already was. "Fair enough. But remember, this city…it offers every kind of fun under the sun. Culture, food, sport, beaches, relaxation, games. Give me a chance and I'll find that one thing that makes it impossible for you to stay away."

Ben's next breath in was deep as he stamped down a ridiculous thought as to one thing that might induce him to pack up and fly halfway across the world. And Nora, she watched him with a sudden woozy fog in her gaze.

She shook it off. And the bright bubbly sunshine girl was back. "Till then, consider this the first of my now daily check-ins!"

I'm about to get this on the daily? he thought,

and something fast and furious, something that felt as if it ought to come with a warning, flickered to life inside him.

"Unless," she said, head cocking to the other side, "you hopped on a plane today. Took the house off my hands. Then you'd never have to hear from me again."

Her smile stretched slowly this time, giving him a flash of tongue before she once again wrapped her lips around the straw.

"Not happening," he said.

"Then I'll talk to you tomorrow." She appeared to slide off the bench, the phone shaking before the connection was lost.

The next afternoon, the new short-term rental agreement Nora had asked Damon to put together landed in her inbox. Despite any stipulations Clancy had put in her will, or Ben's lack of concern about rent, not paying her way just felt wrong.

After their last couple of conversations, it somehow felt even more imperative that when she passed over the keys, it would be a clean break. No ripples, no regrets. Everything on the up and up.

She moved to scrawl her digital signature, before glancing to where Cutie and Pie slept in the corner of her room.

When the Playful Paws crew had suggested

Cutie might encourage Pie out of the shadows, she'd thought it was a ploy. But it had totally worked. They were inseparable. She'd let the foster home know, so they could pick up the pair. Soon.

For now, her top teeth snagged on her bottom lip as she looked back at the part of the contract that stipulated no subletting, no smoking, no illegal activities, no pets.

Officially, they were not her pets. She was only fostering them. Loophole? No. She really should call Ben. Tell him about the dogs. And Clancy's personal patch of happy herbs that still grew in the backyard, which were not illegal so much as they might be a surprise to their new owner.

Tucking her legs up onto her desk chair, Nora grabbed her phone, using the camera as she ran a finger over her teeth, gave her hair a quick fluff. Then she pressed *call*.

When Ben's face snapped onto the screen her breath caught in her throat, as it did every single time she saw the guy. Clean-shaven, eyelashes slightly tangled, dark hair swept into a kind of businessman's quiff—the man really was all kinds of beautiful.

"Hey!" she called, unable to control her goofy grin. So much for only pretending she was softening towards the guy. She could barely keep the warmth from her face, much less the rest of her.

"Nora." A short, sharp, single word of greeting, yet there was a definite smile tilting at his lips. As if maybe Mr McStuffy was softening towards her too.

"Where are you?" she asked, unable to see much behind him bar a grey-tinted window.

"Work."

"What you doing?"

A beat, then, "Work."

"What are you wearing?" The second the words were out of her mouth she regretted them. Then, to press her lack of self-control home, she added, "Have you heard the percentages on how many people who have online work meetings rarely wear pants?"

"I have not."

"Newsreaders do it all the time. Business up top, party on bottom."

Ben's blink was slow, and did things to her insides that made her breath hitch.

"Are you asking me if I'm wearing pants, Ms Letterman?"

"Pfft. No," she scoffed, then ruined the brief moment of cool by saying, "But are you?"

Ben's eyes darkened, just a fraction. Then with a "you asked for it" lift of an eyebrow, he moved his phone slowly down his body.

Past a snow-white shirt, the buttons straining against the broadness of his chest. A conservative red-and-navy-striped tie that fell rakishly to one side. Once he hit the bottom of his shirt, he paused, and Nora held her breath.

Then he swiped the phone over a belt—black, shiny, the buckle brushed silver—and past a pair of very nice suit pants to socks and shoes, the former covered in Batman symbols.

Nora let out her breath in a huff that was half laugh, half relief. What was she expecting? That he was about to put on a peep show? That his socks might be boring? That he might find her assertiveness affronting? That he'd find her, altogether, too much?

Nora was still riddled in discomfort at that last thought when Ben lifted his phone and there was that face again. All rugged angles and dark bedroom eyes. And since her mind's eye was still dealing with the sculpting of that white shirt, the slightly loosened knot of the tie, all the strength that the suit pants beheld, it was a lot.

"Right," she managed to say. "All seems in order, then."

Ben's mouth kicked up at one corner, as if he was fully aware of how flustered she was. And liked it.

That would all come to an end as she was about to tell him about the dogs. And the weed in the garden. And the strange smell coming from the washing machine since she'd washed the dog's blankets.

But first…

"The reason I called, apart from asking when you're coming home…" She waited expectantly.

He gave her a look that made her insides curl and her toes warm.

"Nothing? Okay. Well, I'm about to sign our new rental agreement—"

"Your new what?"

She swung her phone around and showed him the contract on her laptop. "I had Damon draw it up. I insisted. People find me pretty persuasive. Present company excluded."

When she swung her phone back, he looked pained. No, he looked stormy. His voice was preternaturally calm as he demanded, "Show me that again?"

She did as asked. Heard his voice bark, "Were you Clancy's only tenant?"

Funny, she thought, Ben never called Clancy his grandmother. Was it because she'd adopted him? And so late in life? Though, vivacious and vibrant as she was, "grandmotherly" wasn't the first adjective Nora would have used to describe her.

"Nora?"

"Sorry. Yes, I was her only tenant. I rented out the top floor—bed, bath, home office beneath the window. I don't take up much space."

"And *that's* what you were paying?"

When she swung her phone back around, he looked exactly as she'd imagined he might after his first round of emails. Cold, hard, disapproving. The earlier frisson of discomfort felt like mud settling in a hot, heavy ball in her belly, as she felt a confrontation coming on.

She searched her databanks for sparkles, for sunshine, and so unprepared had she been to need it, she came up blank. "Pretty much. Though I asked Damon to up it a little now that I'm not cleaning the place any more. Which is nice. Though who doesn't clean a house before the cleaner comes in, am I right?"

"You asked—" Ben looked ready to pounce, but then he blinked. Blink-blink. The earlier disapproval gone, in a flash. "You were *cleaning* the place for Clancy? As in *cleaning* cleaning?"

"Is there any other kind?"

When he ran a hand over his mouth, and said nothing, she filled the silence.

"I also did the shopping. Looked after the garden. Cooked dinners. Helped host her various community nights. Clancy had company and help, I had affordable room and board. We had eighteen-odd months like that, and it suited us both beautifully."

As her discomfort faded, it made room for indignation. "Which you'd have known if you'd talked to your grandmother more."

"We talked," Ben gritted out. "She simply never mentioned you."

"I find that hard to believe," Nora scoffed,

knowing she was pushing things, but just so glad not to be on the receiving end of bad opinions for a bit.

Ben shifted on his chair, the phone swinging to show a little more of his office. Pale cream walls, huge bookshelves, massive windows—definite Master of the Universe stuff.

"How long?" he asked. "How long was she unwell?"

"What do you mean how long? When did you last speak?"

"A few weeks ago."

"Oh."

Oh, Ben. It had not, not once, occurred to her that *he didn't even know Clancy was sick*. However that miscommunication had come about, whatever their relationship had been, this was *his* family they were talking about. His loss. It was on her to be kind, and gentle, and leave the conversation on even better terms than when she'd started it.

"Not long," she said, her voice softening. "Not long at all. A few weeks. It was... It was really fast. But when the time came, she was ready."

Nora's words drifted between them, like a cloud of smoke after a fireworks display, till Ben broke the silence. "That must have been hard. For you."

His eyes caught on hers, so dark, so deep. It took every bit of willpower she had not to look away. "It was hard. But it was also…a gift. To be there. To the last."

Ben breathed out, his gaze drifting off to the side.

She wondered what he was thinking, what he was feeling, what she might do to make him feel better. But she didn't know him nearly well enough to ask.

"It seems I need to apologise to you, yet again."

"Nah," said Nora, the queen of conciliation. "This is all weird. For both of us."

"Weird is no excuse. I was on the verge of raking you over the coals for taking advantage of an old woman."

"I would never!" Nora spluttered. "I… That's not how I roll."

"I know," he said, his voice a murmur. Then, again, "I know. And I'm sorry."

Nora absorbed those words, that tenuous, unanticipated thread of trust, in that deep rumbling voice; tucking them away in the most special secret memory box she had.

"Clancy, on the other hand—"

He stopped, ran a hand over his whole face, then shifted so that his phone was leaning on something on his desk. On anyone else the angle would give a double chin but Ben just appeared big, and strong, and as if his cape might start fluttering behind him at any moment.

Nora leant elbow on desk and chin on palm and all but sighed.

"I'm not taking any money from you, Nora. If you send the contract back, I'm telling Damon to tear it up."

"It's digital."

Ben breathed out slowly, his expression long-suffering but in a way that didn't set Nora's alarm bells ringing. Instead it felt sort of…intimate. Special.

"Then he will do the digital version of tearing it up."

Nora opened her mouth to reason with him—she really was very good at it.

But then Ben ran a hand through his hair and it reminded her of the times—the many times—people looked pained when she expressed her opinion, or told her she really was too much, and could she just tone the excitement levels down. So she bit her lip and let him be.

"Will you do this for me?" he said.

"Fine," she agreed. "But I will not live here indefinitely. I have plans too, you know!"

"What plans?" he asked, sounding genuinely interested.

"Well, not so much plans as plans to have plans. But I will not overstay my welcome. So you need to get off that pert tushy of yours and get yourself the heck down here!"

Ben's expression stilled, his eyes gazing into hers. "What makes you think my tushy is pert?"

Oops. Um… "I looked you up?"

"Did you?" he drawled. "Chat tomorrow?"

What could she say but, "Count on it!" before quickly hanging up the phone.

Feeling like an emotional taco—tough-looking on the outside, but one bite and her insides would spill out everywhere—Nora let her head fall to the desk.

And promised herself the next time they talked she'd not mention his backside, or his pants.

CHAPTER SIX

"WHERE ARE YOU?" Nora asked Ben, without pre-amble, when he answered the phone a few days and a couple of calls later.

"Work," he said, his phone on speaker.

"Work, work, always work. Why no video?" Nora asked. "Does my expression of disillusion-ment at the fact that *I am still here* make you feel guilty that *you are not here*?"

Ben, who had been reading a scathing email his legal team had drafted to the mediators stall-ing on one small contract negotiation that might tip a fifty-year-old airline into insolvency if it wasn't sorted in the next twenty-four hours, clicked on the camera, and angled the phone against the stapler on his desk.

The screen flickered a moment before Nora's face beamed at him.

Her hair was back off her face, only a couple of loose blonde curls skirting her cheeks. Long, lean golden-brown arms poked out of a white sleeveless T-shirt knotted above her belly button. His next breath in tasted like springtime.

"There you are," she said, with such delight in her voice, in her eyes, he felt it as an ache behind the ribs. Another reason he'd chosen not to use the video.

For things were getting rambunctious between them. *Double entendres* running thick and fast. And he was getting far too used to looking forward to seeing her face. Hearing her voice. Tangling with her wit.

Nora added, "I figured maybe you were, I don't know, getting changed. Or in the shower. Or doing your daily calisthenics and didn't want me to see you in your unitard."

Ben shot her a look, saved the email to draft—he'd finish it later—then grabbed the phone and held it at arm's length, giving her a view of his regular Tuesday suit.

"Ooh," she said, eyebrows waggling. "The money shot."

Ben's laughter was loud enough he looked to the door, to make sure Damon didn't burst in to check he was okay. The kid had been all over him of late. Making sure he was eating. And going home at a reasonable hour. Ben had wondered out loud when he and Damon had married, because he couldn't remember the ceremony, which Damon had thought was the best thing he'd heard all week.

"Where are *you*?" Ben asked.

Nora turned the phone, showing off big silver washing machines and a clean-looking blue-and-white checked floor. "Laundromat."

"Does Clancy not have a washing machine?"

"Did you see the ambience of this place? It's hopping!" she said, glancing away and biting at her bottom lip, a move Ben had come to know was her tell when she was prevaricating.

Ever since Clancy, and the great lie of his life was uncovered, his number one rule in all of his dealings—with employees, clients, friendships—had been honesty. Nora's unpredictability should have provoked him more. But she was just so blatant, his shackles barely quivered.

"Clancy's washer," he repeated.

"Are you asking as my landlord?"

"I am not your landlord; you are staying in Clancy's house as a guest, remember?"

"Good. Because I don't want to tell you how I broke the washer. Not yet."

She pulled her phone closer, till her eyes seemed to fill half the screen. They were a guileless blue, but with just a hint of smoke, much like the woman herself.

Then she said, "You always call her that; did you realise? Clancy. Not Grandma. Or Granny. Was that an adoption thing? Your choice? Hers?"

Ben looked to his office door, suddenly hoping Damon *would* burst through.

Nora continued. "Sorry. That's extra nosey, even for me. Just I... I was a foster kid. Never made it to the adoption phase. Blah-blah-blah. So that kind of thing is seriously fascinating to me."

Despite the fact that her voice was lilting and cheerful, and her eyes were smiling, he caught the yearning beneath. Recognised it. Understood it. Felt another thread of connection to this bright, unusual, relentless woman on the other side of the planet as physically as if a creeping vine had wrapped itself around his middle.

"Forget I asked," she said, her phone shaking as she waved a hand in front of her face. "But give me something. Tell me about the Clancy only you knew?"

Ben sat back in his chair. Hell, maybe if he just came out with it, the whole damn story, she'd understand why he didn't want to go "home". Maybe she'd stop trying so hard to mend things.

Then again, if she gave up on him, he'd never hear from her again.

"She made sure I was well fed," he said, the words coming from some untouched, unbroken place deep inside, "and well read."

Nora's spare hand slapped against her chest. "She constantly plied me books. Though I did the plying with food part."

Something snagged on Ben's subconscious.

Clancy had been a great cook. And she hated people fussing about in her kitchen. Add that to the fact she'd let Nora do the shopping and the gardening…

"*You* cooked for her?"

"I'm quite the amateur foodie. Baking especially, because yum, but I can make a mean main."

Ben nodded, all the while his mind reeled. "Did she ever make you her chilli con carne?"

"Clancy? Are you kidding? She couldn't stomach spicy food. As for cooking, I never even saw her boil an egg."

The snag gave way with a massive yank.

"You said Clancy only found out she was unwell a few weeks ago."

"That's right."

"And how long ago did you move in?"

"Eighteen months or so." Something pinged in the background. "Ooh, washing's done!"

Nora angled the phone against a shelf and proceeded to drag what looked like a set of dragonfly-patterned sheets from the dryer and dump them into a big pink washing basket, leaving Ben to mull over the disquiet that had been whispering at the edges of his mind since he'd seen how little rent Nora had been paying.

Clancy knew. She knew she was sick long before she let on. She'd have hated having a nurse, so instead she opened her home to someone young, and fun, and overconfident. To help. To take care of her. Without giving Nora any warning as to what was to come.

Dammit.

She'd done it again. Lied, outright, to serve her own needs. Without any consideration as to how it might impact the other person. For the rest of their lives.

If he could see Clancy one more time, he'd have some choice words to impart.

Which was likely why she'd never mentioned Nora in their stilted monthly phone calls. The irony too rich, even for her blood.

While Nora continued to empty the dryer, singing something about "a mind at work" under her breath, Ben madly scrambled as to what to say. How to say it. *Whether* to say it. Which made him feel all twisted up inside, as it made him complicit.

"Done!" Nora said, her eyes bright, her hair a little mussed. "Talk tomorrow?"

Ben nodded and Nora hung up.

The image of her grinning at him, soft and sweet and sassy—and totally in the dark—stuck in the back of his mind the rest of the day.

Late the next night, Ben landed on the couch in his lounge with a thud, so spent he didn't even bother taking off his coat.

The apartment was quiet, bar the gentle swoosh of the heating. The double glazing of his wall of windows keeping out the sounds of the city, as well as the rain banging against the outer panes.

He picked up the TV remote and stared at the blank screen, before tossing the remote back onto the coffee table.

Then he glanced to his phone sitting beside him on the couch. It wouldn't ring. *She* wouldn't. Once a day, she had promised, and that was how it had been. And she'd already called that morning.

Yet he found himself waiting for it. Willing it. Wanting to see her face as she flirted up a storm. Or told him stories of the neighbourhood as if it might light up some latent poignancy deep inside him. Or demanded he "come home".

Ben picked up the phone, turned it over and over in his palm. Checked the time in Melbourne. Then he knocked his head against the back of the couch. Once. Twice. Three times. "It's just a phone call. You're a grown-up. You want to call the woman, call her."

And, since she was on the other side of the world and therefore it meant nothing more than a port in a storm, he called.

Nora picked up after several rings.

For once, no bells or whistles or crowds or music added to the show that was Nora Letterman. This time, it was simply her. And, as was becoming habit, her utter loveliness took his breath away.

"Where are you?" he asked without preamble, using the opening line that had somehow become a thing. Their thing. *Port in a storm, my ass.*

She took a beat to take the bait, a beat in which Ben wondered if he'd overstepped. If maybe he was the only one who'd noticed they had "a thing".

But then her face broke into a soft smile. The kind that made his next breath in a little harder to manage.

Her voice was low, unusually subdued as she said, "Home. You?"

"Home."

"You're here?" she asked, clearly not meaning it.

"London. Apartment. The place in which I live. You know, home."

"Ah. That home. Go on, then, give us a look."

"I didn't actually turn the lights on when I came home so all you'd see is the rectangle of light from the microwave clock. Just imagine a minimalist aesthetic. Then take away half the stuff."

"Done," she shot back. Then, yawning wide enough he had a fine view of her tonsils, she tipped onto her side, the phone now taking in a pillow and a dragonfly-patterned sheet over her shoulder.

"You're in bed."

"That I am. While you walked in the door. Sat on the couch. And called me."

Ben was too tired to come up with a better story. "Pretty much."

Again with the soft smile. Again with the tightness in his chest.

"I'm calling because I wanted to make sure you got my package."

"If by package you mean the big, burly dude from the security company who banged on my front door at six this morning, scaring me half to death, to the point I spat out my cornflakes, then yes, I got your package."

He slid down a little lower in the couch, let his feet rest on the coffee table, shoes and all.

"Wait," she said, "I didn't mean *my* front door, I meant *your* front door. I'm just keeping the place warm for you, till you come."

That, Ben thought, had to be the most apt, and loaded, statement of his life. Him here, the heating only just starting to take the edge off the chill of the night. Her, all the way over there, the living embodiment of sunshine.

"So, the package," he said. "It came with a dude?"

"It came with a dude."

"And did that dude fix the alarm system and set you up with a new pass code?"

"Maybe. I didn't ask. I just invited him in and

gave him a bowl of cornflakes. Nice guy. Lactose intolerant, though."

"Nora—"

"Yes. Well. That was the plan. But apparently there's an issue. So he couldn't do it, but he'll be back. I told him there was no rush."

Ben rolled a shoulder and let out a sound that felt something between deep frustration and… whatever this feeling was he always felt when he was talking to Nora. Restlessness. Edginess. As if everything he wanted to say and do was just out of reach.

"Hey, Ben," she said, her mouth mid-yawn, the rough languorous notes in her voice scraping against his insides.

"Yes, Nora."

"I like it when you growl at me."

Ben stopped fidgeting. "Do you, now?"

"Uh-huh," she said, on an outshot of breath, her phone suddenly moving every which way, flashing wall, and wood, and more wall, as if she was changing position. "I do. I do like it."

"And why's that, Nora?"

"Because, Ben, it shows you care."

"Is that right?"

She smiled. Shrugged. And stirred again, the view through the phone flashing and tumbling as she settled into a new position.

Ben ran a hand over his mouth in the effort to

wake himself up, and shifted his legs to make room for a sudden telling discomfort.

It was his own fault; allowing her to control the narrative. She might look as though butter wouldn't melt, but she was astute, and savvy, and not afraid to push his buttons for her own ends, which were different from his own. Something he could pick from a mile away, thanks to Clancy.

That ability had put him light years ahead of the game when starting his own business, but had made interpersonal relationships trickier. He considered himself fair and direct, but had been accused of being hard, cold, unforgiving, his people too in awe of his reputation to offer an opinion contrary to his own.

Which was how he'd let Nora in. She was the antidote. In fact, she'd begun to feel…essential.

"I do care, Ms Letterman," he said, keeping his voice neutral. "I care that the 'dude' I hired will do what I've paid him to do. And can only hope that you were kidding about the cornflakes, in case he's some psycho killer. I'd hate to come home to a crime scene."

"You're coming home?" she asked, her voice husky and laced with hope.

She'd said the same words a thousand times, it was practically the soundtrack to their relationship. But whether it was the darkness of the room, the city lights creating a shimmer out of the corner of his eye, or the slumberous note in her voice, Ben found himself blanketed in the warmth of unexpected, unwarranted, unsought intimacy. And want.

"You're a pushy broad—you know that, right?"

Nora scoffed. "To think I was just starting to like you."

She settled deeper into the pillow till half her face was buried in its softness, her hair now tumbling over her shoulder. His mind went to wondering what it would feel like to be lying there beside her rather than on his stiff couch, mattress sinking beneath him, her warm skin mere inches away.

Bennett breathed in, then out, fully aware that he was well past beginning to like her too.

"Sorry if I've been a little off my usual game," she said through another yawn. "The cornflakes were more of a late-night snack than early brekkie."

Yawning even wider, she covered her mouth with the back of her hand, her palm curling softly towards the phone. It was such a vulnerable thing, the inside of a woman's palm. Secret and warm and intimate. He imagined himself capturing her hand, turning her palm face up. Tracing her lifeline. Pressing his lips to it.

Ben dragged himself back to sitting, the phone pointing at the floor to give himself a break. And he asked, "Big night?"

"A little rough actually."

"How so?"

"Don't worry about it."

"I have nowhere else to be, nothing else to do, but sit here in my big, empty apartment, and listen."

He heard the ragged letting-go of her breath before her voice came to him, monotone and dry. "Matt, one of my foster brothers, called; head in a bad space. I kept him on the phone till his partner was home from her night shift. It's not easy for some, coming from where we came from. Struggling to form relationships, to trust, to believe they deserve to be happy. I'm one of the lucky ones. *Totally* well adjusted."

Her laughter was soft, self-deprecating. Raw.

Ben pressed a thumb into his palm and closed his eyes. For all of her light and loveliness, this was the Nora he found hardest to deny—candid, genuine, vulnerable. If she asked him, right now, to come home, chances were he'd be on a plane by morning.

He turned his phone so that he could see her face once more. His voice was like gravel when he said, "I should let you get some sleep."

"Only if I'm keeping you," she said, her voice coming to him like a memory. "Do you mind if we keep talking for a bit? I don't know why, but hearing your voice somehow makes it seem like everything's going to turn out okay."

Ben nudged his shoes off with his toes, grabbed a cushion and popped it behind his neck as he lifted his legs onto the seat, and lay back. "I can bore you to sleep, if you'd like, by telling you about my day. A day filled with meetings and financial statements and cold takeaway for lunch."

"That sounds just perfect."

And so, Ben kept Nora on the phone, talking about the raindrops slithering down his apartment window, about a girl in the coffee shop downstairs from the office whom Damon had his eye on, about why he liked working with numbers: the clarity, the truth.

"You got a girl out there, Ben?" Nora asked, when Ben stopped talking for a minute.

"No one special," said Ben, his voice starting to grate from overuse.

"Mmm…" Nora murmured, the sound sending waves of sensation rolling through him. "I bet there are plenty who wished they were. The clever ones, who see past your stubborn, grumpy outer shell."

"Dozens," he deadpanned. "Maybe even hundreds. Did you want me to make a list?"

"Sure. Have at it."

A few moments later Nora's phone dropped to the side and all Ben could see was ceiling. All he could hear were her soft even breaths.

And if Ben kept the phone line open for a few minutes while he closed his eyes and let himself rest, and breathe, and be, as he felt the tension of his day slip right away too, no one ever had to know.

CHAPTER SEVEN

BROW TIGHT, SHOULDERS tense as he navigated the heavy crowds spilling out of the shops, Ben took a quick bite of the beef and salad roll he'd nabbed from the Marks & Spencer downstairs, when his phone buzzed in his pocket.

Please let this be good news.

Damon had been instructed to call if they heard from the lawyers, after having put together a tight, last-minute plea to extend credit and hold off a final decision on Metropolis Air's involuntary administration for another six weeks.

Tucking the food under his arm, he juggled the umbrella staving off the misting rain and pulled his phone from his inner jacket pocket. Despite the fact it wasn't the news he was after, warmth skidding through him when he saw Nora's name.

He knew he needed to keep the phone line clear; his thumb still pressed *answer*.

"Where are you?" she said, in a voice of pure sunshine.

"Walking the streets of London."

"No video today? I wore a new hat and everything. Picked it up from Vintage Vamp. It's very fetching."

Ben's cheek tugged. "I can imagine. But while I might have Instagram now, walking and video chatting feels a step too far." He stopped under an awning at the edge of a hidden underground car park, lights flashing as a truck pulled slowly up the driveway. "What can I do for you today, Ms Letterman?"

"Well, Mr Hawthorne, for once this is not a personal call."

The way she said the word *personal* made the warm feeling sizzle a little. Till his wool coat, his double-layered scarf, felt too heavy.

"Business?" he asked. "Or pleasure?"

"Why, Mr Hawthorne," she chastised. "Business, of course."

He imagined her sitting in the swing chair in his office, the view of the Thames a blur behind her, legs crossed, hair tumbling over her shoulders, wearing her new hat, and not much else. Maybe he should be trying to get her to visit him, instead.

"Mate," a voice called behind him, jostling him back to the here and now. The crowd behind him pressed forward and he stepped back into the rain.

"So," Nora's voice continued to sing in his ear. "You know how we talked about you helping

some of my locals with your business amazing-
ness?"

"I remember *you* talking about it."

"Excellent," she said. "The Fleur de Lys florist. Family owned. Their gear is gorgeous. But
their rent is astronomical, a deal they put in place
a decade ago. I thought, perhaps, you might rep-
resent them in their renegotiations."

"Unfortunately, my team has to turn more clients away than we are able to take on."

"Really, Mr Big Shot?"

"I'm not tooting my own horn, Nora. I'm
merely pointing out my business model. I don't
offer myself to clients, they come to me."

"Huh. And there I was, thinking you were
some ambulance chaser. Was it the cheap hair-
cut, perhaps? Or the polyester suits?"

The feet ahead of him kicked dirty puddle
water onto his Savile Row suit pants, yet he
couldn't help smiling. Laughing really, at his
own hubris. Nora had a way of making everything he'd ever believed about himself shift. Just
a little. Just enough. To think that maybe there
might be, could be, more out there than the life
he'd built.

"Then there's also the local restaurant," she
went on. "Ambrosia. I think their chef enjoys
the fact he's spending other people's money. Last
time I spoke with the owner he looked like he'd
aged a hundred years. When I mentioned I knew

a guy who was a whizz with finances he practically fell to his knees in gratitude."

Ben turned the corner, the entrance to The Shard in sight.

"You'll do it, right?" she asked. "I can send Damon their contact details? Hmm? Hmm? Dust off that invisible cape of yours?"

Before he could reiterate the impossibility of her request, Bennett was bumped from behind, his wrap knocked free, landing half open on the ground. Phone pressed against his ear, he scooped up the mess and tossed it into the closest rubbish bin.

"Ben?"

"I'm here," he said. "I'm just…" Wet, filthy and hungry. Lost. "Just wondering what the weather's like there."

A beat, then, "Well, I'm looking outside my little office window in the apartment upstairs, and it's around ten o'clock-ish at night here. So it's dark. But clear. Clear enough I can see a couple of stars, despite the streetlamps and the night lights from all businesses across the road. How about where you are?"

Ben, now an island amidst a churning sea of wet, grumbling Londoners, tipped his head back and his umbrella with it, letting the misting rain soak him through. But he also caught the sun, its weak glow shining beyond the smear of grey covering the sky. The same sun that would beam down on her, blue and sunny and warm, in a few short hours.

The urge to say, *I'm booking a flight today* filled his throat. Right alongside, *What the hell am I doing getting wet like this? I must be going mad.*

He closed his umbrella and ran the last few metres till he was under the protection of The Shard's entryway. "I'm fine," he said. Then adjusted it to, "Send me those details, okay?"

"Really? Oh, my gosh, Ben. You are the best. The absolutely most wonderful best. I could just kiss you! Or maybe hug you. Or shake your hand vigorously at the very least. When might that be possible, do you think?" she asked, her voice suddenly a little husky.

"The shaking of my hand?" he asked. The doorman smiled politely as Ben passed, as if he didn't look like a drowned rat.

"Sure. That."

The air-conditioning bled through his wet suit, hitting his skin like a sudden snowstorm. "The florist and the restaurant. Let's start there."

"Okay."

There was a pause, then Ben stretched his ears to hear her say, "Bye, Ben."

"Goodbye, Nora."

When the lift doors closed he was surprised to find a bedraggled giant looking back at him, with a moony grin on his face.

* * *

Nora sat on one of the upholstered cane chairs in the sunroom at the back of the house; a blanket over her knees, sipping on her first cup of coffee of the day.

When her phone rang, Ben, her first thought was: *Better than coffee.* Which, even in the depths of her early morning state, she knew was a problem.

"Where are you?" he asked, the moment she pressed *answer*. Lights flickered behind him; city buildings through a rainy window. His face was all hard-carved shadows in the darkness of what she assumed was his apartment late at night.

"The sunroom." Nora checked to make sure Cutie wasn't nearby—she hadn't quite got around to sending him back or telling Ben—then panned the camera around the room.

Sunshine poured through the white shutters, sending shafts of creamy gold over the soft wood floor, the chairs, the jewel-coloured throws and cushions.

"Go back," Ben's voice commanded from the speaker of the phone.

"What? Which bit?" she asked, with a flare of excitement that something about the house had caught his curiosity.

"To the bit that looked like your underwear drying in the corner."

Nora turned the camera back to her face. "Seriously? There's nothing to see. It's basic boyfriend undies in whatever colour is on sale."

"Eye of the beholder," Ben said, waggling his eyebrows.

Nora snorted. The guy was in a good mood. It suited him.

"So how about you?" she asked.

"You want to see what underwear I prefer?"

"It's okay. You can just tell me. Y-fronts? Chastity belt? Woollen tights?"

"Why not commando?"

At that Nora burst into laughter. Ben really was in a mood. And it really was better than coffee. Just thinking his name made her blood warm, and her skin tingle. She was long since past the realisation that she'd developed quite the crush on Ben Hawthorne.

The fact that he lived a million miles away? The best kind! Ben *wasn't* coming home, not any time soon, so she could indulge in all the lovely daydreams, but none of the hope, or the heartache. A crush on Ben Hawthorne was safe as houses.

"What exactly is it about me that makes the thought of my going commando so hilarious?" Ben asked.

"You are kidding, right? I'd be more likely to go commando than you. In fact, I have, more than once, when I've waited too long for laundry day. And why do I keep telling you things that I would never tell another living soul?"

There was a long pause. "I feel like this conversation has spun a little off topic."

"Oh, so you *didn't* call so that we might talk underwear?"

"Shockingly, no."

The lighting changed as he switched on a lamp. No, he'd opened the fridge door; his face all angles and beauty in the cool light. Nora's heart thumped and shimmied in her chest.

"Just quickly, I've been talking to some of your friends," said Ben, his eyes roving back to hers. "The restaurant. The florist."

Nora sat up so fast the blanket on her knees fell to the floor. "Ben! Oh, my gosh. Could you help them?"

"I believe I already have. Now, it might surprise you to find I am not a fan of the social media."

"No?"

"But the upswing in custom both businesses saw after taking you on was marked. You're very good at what you do. So I've told them they need to do whatever it takes to keep you around."

Nora's belly flipped. Then flopped. It might have been one of the nicest things anyone had ever said to her, but it had a heartbreak chaser. Staying wasn't an option. A girl couldn't be footloose and fancy-free if she had connections all over the place, constantly tugging on her heart.

"I concur, I really am quite amazing. But still, it's nice of you to say."

"My pleasure."

"But just to be sure, you have other ways to help them, right? You're not relying entirely on me—"

"You can park the panic, Nora. I have. I will."

"Right. Great."

There was a pause. A pause in which she held her breath, waiting for him to sign off, yet hoping he would not. Not yet.

Then he said, "I think this might be the longest time you've gone without asking when I'm coming home."

"When are you coming home?" she asked, her voice deadpan.

His laugh was a deep, sexy rumble. And then he rang off.

Nora kept the phone cradled in her hands as if it might help keep the warm, fuzzy feelings tucked all around her.

Crushes were nice, she decided. She might even do this on the regular. With other people. Once the whole Ben Hawthorne saga was done and dusted. Though when she tried to picture someone, anyone, she'd ever met filling that void, she came up blank.

It was bizarre to think that when Clancy was

alive, Ben had barely registered as a person in her head.

Then he'd morphed into the bad guy in Clancy's tale. A terrible grandson; selfish, ungrateful, even cruel. Somehow worse, in Nora's mind, because he'd been adopted, when she'd never had that chance.

But now when she thought of Ben—and she thought of him far more often than was in any way sensible—she knew that he was many things. Wry, generous, conflicted, strong-minded, too handsome for his own good, a workaholic. A man who'd dedicated his life to getting people out of trouble. A man, she was beginning to believe, who was rather lonely out there in the big city.

A confidant.

A friend.

Whatever had happened between him and Clancy no longer felt as if it had quite so much to do with her. She'd surprised herself by discovering she had room inside her for liking them both.

But still, it was just a crush. Nothing so perilous, so terrifying, as actual feelings. Her heart had been far too beaten down by rejection to ever let that happen.

Late Friday afternoon, the stay on the Metropolis Air insolvency had been granted.

It meant Hawthorne Consultancy had breathing space: six weeks in which to plug the leaks, make a plan to repay creditors, and create the bones of a new business model that would keep the airline's staff in employment and their planes in the air.

Nora was right: cape or no cape, helping people did feel good. Turned out the joy in what he did wasn't just about the numbers, after all.

Speaking of Nora, when he'd heard the news she was the first person he'd wanted to tell. Part of him was thankful it was the middle of the night in Melbourne, forcing him to pull his head in and make plans with his team, instead. That had to be his focus, now.

And yet, come Saturday morning, Ben once again felt restless. So restless he'd tossed and turned all night. Which was how he found himself heading into the office late Saturday afternoon, his head filled with mad plans he couldn't possibly air.

When the lift doors opened on the twenty-fifth floor, he paused at the sound of chatter. Peering around the door, Ben found the place abuzz, with several desks in use.

Carly—a go-getter, second-year paralegal, and the assistant he'd had on rotation just before Damon—saw him and stood to attention, hair in a high ponytail, decked out in running gear. Her gaze widened, dropped and lifted; she was clearly discombobulated by the sight of the boss in jeans, jumper and coat.

"Mr Hawthorne!" she cried, and a ripple went through the place, heads popping out from all over, the chatty noise hushing. "We didn't think we'd see you till Monday."

"I could say the same about you. What's going on?"

"Um…"

"Why's it so quiet in here?" That was Damon, heading around the corner with phone in one hand, a coffee in the other. "Oh. Hey, boss. Didn't think we'd see you here till Monday."

"We've done that bit already."

Carly leapt out from her cubicle. "Don't blame Damon. When he came to us, asking if we'd be keen to get some extra experience on a big account, by helping the Metropolis team get a head start on the grunt work, we leapt at the chance."

Another paralegal added, "You work so hard, Mr Hawthorne."

Carly nudged back in front of her second and added, "And it's come to our attention that, while HR insists *we* take our leave in a timely manner, none of us have seen you do the same. Which doesn't seem fair."

Ben looked over the crowd of young faces, before he found Damon once again, at the back of the small crowd, leaning against a cubicle. "It came to your attention, did it?"

Damon lifted his coffee in salute.

Carly popped up onto her toes. "The next

couple of weeks are all about data processing, collation, reporting, finding discrepancies and obvious areas of improvement. The grunt work. Right?"

"That's right." Funnily enough, it was exactly what he'd been thinking all night long.

"*We* can do that," Carly insisted.

"I know you can," Ben allowed. "It's why I hired such a bright, self-motivated, energetic team, after all."

Carly grinned at her counterparts, who all grinned back.

Damon—who had ambled over to the group of eight or ten staff who had now collected around Carly's desk—added, "Leaving you free to swoop in like Superman and save the day at the last."

Carly turned and glared at Damon. Then looked from boss's assistant to boss, as if only just figuring out she was a pawn in someone else's game. "This is not a coup," she said, "if that's what you're worried about."

"Well, it hadn't been..." said Ben, finding himself laughing. For a strange feeling of lightness had come over him. A mix of relief and possibility. "Truly, though, you guys have blown me away. Now, you can all go home, enjoy what's left of the weekend, and come back fresh and ready to tackle this on Monday. You, on the other hand—" Ben pointed a finger at his assistant "—come with me."

Ben made a beeline for his office, where he went straight for the safe tucked behind a picture of a sailing boat on his wall. And he didn't much care for boats.

A designer had chosen it. The same one who'd decked out his apartment. And he'd let them. As it allowed him to live like an automaton. Work, home. Work, home. Too busy working, proving himself, building a reputation for honesty and impeccable work, to even pick a comfortable couch.

He'd built a fortress of self-protection. As if getting *comfortable* would leave him open to attack, vulnerable to having his life tumbling down around his ears. Again.

And it was a lonely place to be.

"You might be looking for this."

Out of the corner of his eye, Ben saw Damon holding out Ben's passport. And a dossier.

Damon wandered into the office. "List of daily flights to Melbourne, a map of Melbourne with the address of your grandmother's house circled in red, some Aussie cash, and your passport. I've had it ready for the last week."

Ben carefully took the dossier from Damon's hand. "I'm not sure if you're the best assistant I've ever had, or if I should change the locks."

Damon grinned. "Figure it out later. After your holiday."

Ben's fingertips pressed hard into his palm,

as if trying to alert him to the fact he might be about to do something uncalculated. With too many variables to control. Something bonkers.

He uncurled his fingers, knowing all of that and wanting to go anyway. Needing to go. It was time. "Set up a meeting with the heads of department for Monday."

"Emails are drafted, letting them know you're taking time off. No meeting necessary. I press *send*, you're good to go."

"So, it is a coup."

Damon grinned. Then followed Ben out of the office door.

In between staff members calling out, "Have a good break!"

"Get a tan!"

"Bring back some sunshine!"

Ben told Damon, "I might be out of town, but I still require constant updates. You be my firewall. Filter as you need to. I trust you."

Damon's next smile held none of its usual cockiness. "Thanks, boss. Fair warning, there might be a slight bump in doughnut purchases to keep this ragamuffin bunch going, but with my new title and company card I can take that on."

"And what title is that?"

"Permanent attachment to the Desk of Bennett J Hawthorne."

"You want to *remain* as my assistant?" Ben asked as he moved into the lift, slapping the dossier against his palm, feeling the telling bump of his passport.

"For now. So I can learn at the feet of the master. Because in the long term, I plan to *be* you. I'll keep your seat warm while you're gone."

Ben's laughter echoed as the lift doors closed.

CHAPTER EIGHT

NORA'S EYES HAD just started to drift shut, the Harlan Coben book she was reading tipping precariously towards her nose, when she was startled awake at the sound of a knock at the front door.

A few woozy blinks and a glance at the clock on her phone told her she still had a couple of hours for a last tidy before the cleaner came. It was likely someone selling electricity plans.

Having stayed up way too late re-watching the entire second season of *Fleabag* for the zillionth time, then spending the morning preloading a bunch of content for a couple of local businesses before tying off their contracts, a nap was necessary.

She rolled over, laid her arm over her eyes and—

Knock-knock-knock.

"Argh! Okay!" she shouted, sitting up so fast her head spun.

Dragging herself out of bed, Nora tugged at

her vest top—it would do—then grabbed a pair of ancient cut-off denim shorts from the top of her clean-clothes pile and dragged them over her undies.

Knock. Knock-knock!

"Sheesh. I'm coming!" Nora called, twirling her wild hair into a messy bun atop her head as she jogged down the precariously skinny stairs.

At the door she checked to make sure Cutie wasn't about—he had a habit of licking door-knockers half to death—then she opened the front door a crack.

Only to swing it open wide when she found Bennett Jude Hawthorne standing on Clancy's front porch.

"Oh, my God. You're here!" she blurted.

"That I am," he said in a voice that—up close, in person—was, if possible, deeper than over the phone. Lit with a loose, lackadaisical drawl.

The backs of Nora's knees began to tingle, while her feet felt as if they weren't quite attached to her body.

Because *he* was there. He was really there! He wasn't merely a warm voice on the phone, or a two-dimensional image on a screen, or some impossible crush she could happily indulge as he lived on the other side of the planet.

He was here. He was real. And, boy, was he beautiful.

There was no other word for it.

Misty hadn't been kidding when she called him mountainous, for the man was tall. With serious shoulders filling out a brown suede jacket, all kinds of heft filling out dark jeans, and if his boots weren't kidding his feet were huge. Add thick, dark, wavy hair with a perfect smattering of silver over his ears she'd never noted before, and those intense eyes; the man oozed fire-crackling, log-cabin-on-a-winter's-night deliciousness.

Nora shook her head, feeling as if she were coming out of a trance. "When did you get in? Did I miss a call?"

"The decision was made. I got on a plane. I am a man of action. When I want to be." With that came a smile. A lazy kick at one corner of his beautiful mouth.

Holy moly. Nora was tingling so hard it was a miracle she didn't set on fire.

"Come in!" she said, a small measure of sense finally finding a way through the fog that had overcome her. "*Mi casa, su casa.* Literally."

With that, her mind stuttered back to reality. She remembered the kitchen she was yet to clean before the cleaner came, the clothesline still covered in undies and bras she'd set up by the sunny window in the sunroom out back, the dogs—

The dogs! She'd yet to tell Ben about the dogs. Or, you know, make sure they didn't live here any more, as per his landlordy stipulations.

She cocked an ear, but couldn't hear the tell-tale tick-tick-tick of Pie's claws on hard wood, or Cutie's desperate whimpers. Meaning they must be out back stalking a bird or digging up the garden. For now.

Still, what could she do but step back, swoosh an arm towards the hallway like a game-show host, and wait for him to pass?

The scents of the outdoors came with him as he entered the house, jasmine and myrtle, as well as something other. Something warm and rich and wholly delicious. Him.

Nora shut the door and leaned against it, using its solidity to keep her grounded as Ben Hawthorne filled the entrance. With his bigness and his elegance and his delicious scent.

He didn't go far, the back of his head moving as he seemed to take the place in. Fair enough too. Everything he saw was now his.

Well, not everything. Not *her*.

"Has the place changed much, since last you were here?" she asked, her voice sounding not at all as if she had lemonade in her veins.

"Not a bit," said Ben, his voice gruff.

Then he turned, shooting her a quick smile. When his eyes caught on hers, they darkened all the more. All the air seemed to disappear from the room.

Nora's stomach swooped. Her heart thudded in her throat.

Ben.

He was *right there*. Within touching distance. Big, overwhelmingly beautiful, smelling like the woods in springtime, and looking at her as if he was rather taken by the fact she was within touching distance too.

"It seems I've caught you unawares," he said, a definite hint of humour lighting his velvety voice.

"What? No. It's all good. I'm fine. I was just—" She turned, flapped a hand towards the stairs, and her messy bun flopped sideways, a hank landing in her eye. She swished it back over her shoulder and held a hand to her face. "I have pillow marks on my cheek, don't I?"

"Pillow—?"

"I was napping, see. Yes, in the middle of the day. Because I can. I'm decadent, that way. One of the joys of being footloose and fancy-free." By habit she held out her arm, showing off her tattoo.

His eyes followed the move, took it in, before they dropped to her bare legs, slid smoothly over her tank top, under which she remembered she was not wearing a bra, then back to her face.

Nora pulled her arm across her belly, suspecting her distraction-by-sunshine move might not have near the same impact it usually did. Not with this man. This astute, acute, grown-up man.

"This is weird, right? I mean, I'm not sure whether I should shake your hand or…" *or throw myself into your arms, bury my face in your neck and breathe you in till I faint* "...or hug you."

Ben breathed in, breathed out, and said nothing.

"So it's just me," she managed. "Good to know. If you don't mind, I'll duck up and get dressed."

"Not at all," he said. Though something in his voice made her think he'd prefer she stayed. Just as she was.

Breathless, light-headed, in need of a moment to reset, Nora moved past him, quickly breathing in his warm rich scent—like a sip from a sneaky flask at a dry wedding—before bolting up the stairs.

"Coffee machine is on!" she threw over her shoulder. "I baked, late last night, so there are snacks. I won't be a minute!"

She hit the bedroom at a run, caught sight of herself in the mirror. Face pink, tiny curls framing her cheeks, eyes overbright. Nipples saying, *Why, hello, Ben...* beneath her thin white vest.

Oh, good gravy.

She found some floaty linen pants, a loose top, a bra, and hustled them on. She gave her hair a quick finger-detangle before twisting it into a loose side plait. Swiped on a little lip gloss. Tidied up her mascara. Gargled a minty mouthwash—

Then stopped.

She closed her eyes and breathed. Told herself to calm the heck down.

Ben was not here *for* her. *Maybe* something she'd said had helped him make the decision to come home, to claim his inheritance, but that was the extent of her involvement.

But he was here. Meaning her promise to Clancy had been fulfilled. She could grab her bag, right now, do the rounds of the neighbourhood, say her goodbyes, and go.

Anywhere. Land where she landed. Find a small patch of space for herself in a share house, or a motel. And start over. Start fresh. No expectations.

But something inside her tugged. Something unfinished.

If she gave herself just a *little* more time, maybe she could do more. Help Ben make peace with his wonderful grandmother. Then she could walk away from this whole experience, truly free and clear.

Nothing left undone. No regrets. No looking back.

On the way out of the door she spotted Cutie and Pie's day bed in the corner. She grabbed an old throw from the back of her office chair, tossed it over the dog bed, and headed downstairs.

Ben didn't move.

He could hear Nora moving around upstairs—

footsteps, drawers opening, taps turning on and off. But he stayed where he stood, his hand gripped tight to the handle of his suitcase, his shoes glued to the floor.

For his senses were being bombarded with memories of his sneakers squeaking on the dark wood floors, counting the blown bulbs in the ancient chandelier, running his hands over the wallpaper every time he walked into the kitchen...

Despite Nora's belief Clancy couldn't boil an egg, the galley kitchen, with its wooden doors and dark green marble bench tops, was the room in which Clancy had spent much of her time while he was growing up: cooking Vietnamese salads, American burgers, Italian pasta sauces from scratch. He could almost smell the herbs, even now.

But then his throat tightened, the backs of his eyes gritty, as he remembered the first time he'd braved asking Clancy about his birth parents. She'd gripped the kitchen bench, her eyes haunted, her voice reed thin as she'd asked: wasn't he happy there with her? Hadn't she given him a wonderful life?

"Hey," a voice called from behind him.

Ben flinched so hard his shoulder tweaked.

He took a moment to centre himself before he turned to find Nora at the bottom of the stairs, a hand resting on the railing.

From the moment he'd had his passport in his

hand, he'd been on a forward trajectory. Book flight, pack bag, connect with heads of department to make sure they all knew this wasn't a fortnight in the Bahamas. He was contactable. He was on the clock.

Then suddenly he was standing outside Clancy's gate. The scent of jasmine near overwhelming. He'd been so cocky, so gung-ho, he hadn't considered how it might feel to be back, knowing Clancy wasn't there, and never would be again.

He'd walked to the front door on legs of lead. His arm not feeling like his as he'd knocked.

Then Nora had opened the door, and everything else had just melted away.

A vision of long brown limbs, sleep-softened face, and joy. Behind the surprise, she'd been truly happy to see him. Knowing it, feeling it, some deep, lawless part of him had unfurled under the regard of those big blue eyes. At the sight of a bare foot running up and down the back of her calf. The way her breaths had become deep and hard won.

It had occurred to him in that moment, the hold she had over him. The place she had made for herself in his head. If he wasn't careful, he could get into a lot of trouble for this woman.

"Okay!" she said, clapping her hands, her eyes not quite meeting his. "Let's start over, get you settled in. As you know, I have the apartment upstairs, but can move my stuff out in five minutes. Or the spare room beside the sitting room is made up. Or there's Clancy's room—"

"Spare room is fine," he gritted out. His old room. Clancy had assured him when he'd first moved out, to go to university, it would be called "Ben's room" until the end of time. Another equivocation in a long line of them.

"Okay, then," said Nora.

Her eyes finally found his and a frisson of electricity, of heat, seemed to arc through the air. Connecting them. As if the bond he'd felt from, oh, so far away had been amped up to eleven.

She took an audible fortifying breath as she slid past him, as if that might negate the disrupting crackle of attraction. His feet finally moved, following hers.

When she hit his old bedroom door, Nora nudged it open, then stood in the doorway, her hands tucked behind her, her body at one with the doorjamb.

As Ben moved past Nora, he could feel the air around her shift. Could taste citrus at the back of his throat. Could feel a burst of sunshine on his wrist closest to her.

Thus unnerved, he entered the spare room to find small aeroplanes swooping over dark walls. The ceiling pale grey with fluffy white clouds. The chest of drawers sporting a small collection of stickers saved from the apples he'd eaten over the years. It was a time capsule, after all.

"I'll leave you be—" said Nora, her voice tugging him back from the brink of near desperate discomfort.

"No," he said, tossing his suitcase and jacket on the single bed and running both hands through his hair in an effort at keeping himself in the here and now. "I'd rather stay awake. Fight the jet lag. How about a tour?"

"Of the house?" she asked, eyes narrowing. "Trying to make sure I haven't done off with the family candlesticks?"

"If there are any, you're welcome to them."

Her laughter was bright, and big. "Nah. I'm good."

Nevertheless, she bowed to his request, taking him through the house, telling charming tales about her time there, and using the chance to talk up Clancy: how beloved she was in the community, her wild style, her wicked sense of humour.

The fact that she was as transparent in person as she was over the phone eased something inside him. She was the woman who'd drawn him here. Who he'd hoped to find when he'd stepped up to the front door.

"Keeping in mind you gave me no time to tidy up, you're welcome to check out the apartment upstairs," she said, suddenly finding her fingernails fascinating.

"But, Nora, we've just met."

Her gaze lifted to his, a wild spark glinting

within the smoky blue. "Ha-ha." Then she took the first step, then the second, all but daring him to follow. "You've already seen my underwear, so I have nothing to hide. Come on up if you dare."

Ben dared, having to turn his feet at an angle so as not to trip.

Once upstairs her bravado faltered as she quickly swept him past her unmade bed—he felt himself smiling at the sight of the dragonfly sheets. One pillow sat neat and trim at the head of the bed, the other at an odd angle, comforter askew, as if she was a restless sleeper. The bathroom smelt of fruity shampoo, and soft soap, and skin. Of Nora.

"So that's it! Shall we…head back downstairs?" she asked, her voice lifting at the end, as if there was an alternative.

Ben took the initiative, moving out of the door, but not before sending her a feral grin that made her cheeks pink, even as she rolled her eyes.

Halfway down the stairs, his big feet turned so he didn't fall off the edge, Ben stopped, turned, checked to see she was coming.

She was. Right behind him. With a loud, "Whoop!" she tried to stop her descent, her hands landing on his shoulders to steady herself.

But gravity had its own ideas.

Ben's big feet, not having purchase, slipped down a step, or two. Ben grabbed her, spinning so that they didn't both tumble down the damnable stairs. Even so, they landed awkwardly, her body sprawled on top of his, his face buried in her hair.

In the quiet that followed, Ben did a quick mental scan, assessing the damage to body and limb. Her breath washed over his ear as she huffed out a laugh, sending goosebumps shooting down his neck, and it was all he could feel.

"You okay?" he asked, his voice rough, his hands moving over her shoulder, her skull, swiping her hair from her eyes.

She nodded, her hair sliding through his fingers. Her body shifting, rubbing up against him in a most unfortunate way if he wanted to get out of this with his dignity intact.

"Are *you*?" she asked.

"I'm fine," he said, his voice rough.

Her eyes flickered between his before her gaze dropped to his mouth. Meaning she didn't miss a syllable as he growled, "Now you have me here, what do you plan to do with me?"

Her eyes shot back to his. Wide. Filling with heat, with smoke.

"In Melbourne," he qualified, shifting a little to ease the feel of a step digging into his back, only to have the length of her slide more fittingly over his. "It's been your mission to get me here. I'm here. So now what?"

"I can feed you," she said, her chest rising and

falling, eyes once again locked on his mouth. "Or we can head out for a bite."

"I could eat," he said. "Either way."

When her eyes moved back to his, her pupils had all but swallowed the oceans of blue.

"Unless," he said, barely in control of his own voice any more, "you have something better in mind?"

Later, he couldn't be sure who moved first, but next thing he knew her mouth was on his. Hot, wet and wanton.

Somehow they moved, till she was lying back on the stairs, Ben over the top of her. Her hands were tugging on his shirt till she found skin. Splaying across his back, kneading, hauling him closer, waves of heat rocketing through his body while his hands were buried deep in her silken hair as they kissed. And kissed. And kissed. No teasing, no testing; wet, lush, exquisite.

When his tongue swept into her mouth and she groaned, he saw stars. Moons. Distant constellations.

As if the weeks of conversation, flirtation, of building sexual tension, of play, of talking late into the night, falling asleep to one another's yawns and husky goodnights, had been long-build foreplay that had funnelled them here, to this moment.

Then Ben's knee hit a stair, sending a sharp shot of pain up his leg, right as he heard something of hers hit the wood with a loud *thunk*. Her elbow, he realised when her head dropped back to lean on the stair and she dragged her arm between them to give her elbow a rub.

Ben shifted, giving her room. Himself too. Even as he found himself in all kinds of discomfort—from bumps and bruises and tightness in the front of his pants. Her eyes were scrunched closed, even as she laughed, the sound husky and raw, and sexy as all get out.

"What were we thinking?" she asked.

"I wasn't."

More laughter. He did love her laugh.

The pain eased from her face and her eyes fluttered open. "This kind of thing always looks so hot in movies."

"Which movies? Tell me their names."

Nora laughed again, and it felt as if diamonds were exploding behind his ribs. It was ridiculous. Reckless. Irresistible. His fingers of his right hand were near enough to her wild braid, he let them get lost in a loose curl before giving it a light tug.

Then her knee shifted, sliding between his legs, making contact with a gentle insistent nudge. Before he had the chance to draw breath her body followed, undulating into him, all soft curves and bumptious invitation.

It was enough to bring him back to reality.

Giving her one last smile, he carefully pressed

himself to standing then held out a hand to help her do the same.

She took his hand and curled herself upright. Standing two steps above him, she was nearly eye to eye. This woman, a walking, talking peril.

"I knew these stairs were a danger. I'd asked Damon to look into my liability in case anything happened."

"This what you had in mind?"

He'd not had *any* of this in mind back then. Not an unplanned trek to Australia. Not facing Clancy's legacy. And certainly not Nora Letterman.

She reached out and tugged the neckline of his shirt back into place, her small light hands running over his chest. Then she grabbed a hunk of shirt and tugged him towards her.

Her vivid gaze remained glued to his. Her tongue darted out to wet her top lip before her teeth dragged over the plump lower lip. Slowly, incrementally closing the gap; this time, giving both of them the chance to decide if this was a mistake.

By the time her lips met his she was trembling. Hell, maybe it was him.

Either way, if their first kiss had been an explosion of flint and steel, this was a slow, soft exploration. Her lips dragging over his. Again and again. Finding where she fitted best. His arm slid around her waist, bringing her closer, as if in slow motion; so that when her body finally lined up against his he could almost feel the house sigh in relief.

Eons later, when she pulled back, her eyes were closed. Ben turned her till her back was against the wall; his hand braced beside her head, determined not to let the stairs, or gravity, get the best of him.

She lifted her hand to her lips, then she murmured, as if to herself, "I've been wondering what that might feel like for the longest time. You feel like lunch yet?"

Lunch. Ben needed a moment to fathom the meaning of the word.

"Or," she said, lifting her head, to whisper against his ear, "we could go back upstairs."

The hand against the wall curled into the wallpaper. Hell, this was fast. He'd been in her vicinity fifteen minutes, tops. But the truth was, they'd been a snowball rolling down a hill, gaining speed and momentum, since their very first conversation.

Yet, he was no savage, prone to act on a whim. He made decisions based on reason, evidence, fact. One of them had to try to take control of this thing.

"We should slow down," he managed.

"Why?"

Good question.

"I'm a big girl, Ben. And you are most certainly a big boy. Whatever worries are bouncing about inside that big brain of yours, let them go. I am the one thing in your life that you never, ever have to worry about. I ask nothing of you but this. Now."

She took him by the hand and moved a step higher, tilting her head towards the upstairs apartment, towards her big, soft bed, giving him that slow, languorous, wider-than-should-be-possible smile, and he thought, *To hell with it*.

He was on holiday, after all. For the first time in more years than he could count, he was responsible for no one but himself.

At the letting go Ben felt something shift inside him. Something big and cumbersome and weighty. He felt a hook slide into the new-found space, right through his centre, tugging him wherever Nora chose to take him.

Which was up the stairs, and into her bed.

Skin still slick with sweat, bones lax, muscles no longer of any use, her entire body drifting on a blissful fog, Nora stared at a spot on the ceiling where a small patch of paint was flaking away, as her thoughts threatened to spin out into crazy town.

She'd just taken Ben Hawthorne to bed. Literally taken him by the hand and led him there! What had she been thinking? She *hadn't*. That much was clear.

And what happened to helping Ben make

peace with his wonderful grandmother so she could walk away, no regrets?

One thing she hadn't considered when letting her feelings for Ben have free rein, while they'd flirted, and teased, and talked about things she never talked about with anyone, ever, was that within the word *crush*, crushing was implied. *Being* crushed. The heaviness she felt in her chest sure felt as if it was heading that way.

When Ben moved beside her, all big and warm and strong, Nora whimpered; the urge to curl into him, absorb his warmth, absorb *him*, was rich and lush and terrifying.

She flopped her arm over her eyes, as if that might quell out the tumble of concerns fast bubbling up inside her.

"Nora," Ben murmured, in that deep, rumbling, bone-melting voice of his. "Everything okay over there?"

"Mmm-hmm," she said, her voice coming out an octave too high. "Everything's super-duper!"

Nora felt Ben's fingers—oh, God, those fingers—curl around hers, before he gently lifted her arm away from her face. She gave herself a moment, or three, to brace herself against the onslaught of that face before she opened her eyes to find him leaning on one elbow, looking down on her.

Her heart *kerthunked*. Her head swooned. His

heartbreaker face was just so serious, and earnest, and lovely, it made her ache.

"That was my fault," she blurted.

"How so?"

Excellent question. "Okay, maybe it was your fault for smelling so good."

His mouth kicked ever so slightly at one corner, as if he was laughing at her—no, as if he was *delighted* by her—and it was possibly the most beautiful thing she'd ever seen.

"If so," he said, lifting a hand to his chest, his beautifully sculpted chest, "then I take full responsibility."

Nora smiled. Dreamily. Then shook her head hard enough her brain *thunked* against the sides of her skull. "See, now you're looking at me as if I'm adorable. But you should know, I'm this delightful to everyone. So don't think you're special."

"I wouldn't dare."

"Actually," she went on, as if he hadn't spoken, "maybe not *that* delightful. The falling-into-bed part was new. An aberration. A hiccup."

"A hiccup," he repeated, though he didn't seem at all perturbed by her summation. Instead his fingers curled around a lock of her hair. Then he leaned down and placed a kiss on her cheek, then another at the edge of her ear.

Her eyes closed and she let out a sigh, her body shifting as waves of pleasure scooted through her. If she wasn't careful, if she didn't get control of herself, she'd be hiccupping again before she knew it.

"The cleaner!" she cried, eyes flying open.

"What about her?"

"Him. He's due soon. Any minute."

"Okay." His lips moved down her neck, dragging against the skin till she felt feverish.

"He has a key!"

Ben's mouth halted. He laid one more kiss on her collarbone, as if he was marking his place with a promise, then he sat back up.

Nora did the same, bringing the sheet with her. The rest barely covered Ben, hip to thigh; his huge feet hung off the end of the mattress.

Oh, now you're all demure, a devil on her shoulder intoned. *Five minutes ago you were riding him like a—*

"As I was saying," she blurted, "what happened, just now, was the result of a number of factors."

"My smell, your adorableness…"

"Yes. And hanky-panky can be wonderfully… ah…*distracting.*"

He blinked, his long-angled lashes sweeping against his cheeks. The move devastating to any kind of balance she might be trying to regain. "Distracting."

"Sure. We clearly both needed a good…distraction. From how much we both miss Clancy."

At that, Ben reared back, his brows coming together, forming deep burrows in his forehead. Seriously? How could forehead burrows be so sexy? But, gosh, they were.

He ran a hand over his face, before saying, "Don't do that."

"Do what?"

"Negate what happened by making it about Clancy." His voice sounded weary. None of the delicious, teasing burr that had kept her enthralled as he'd whispered all the things he'd imagined doing to her during their late-night phone calls, then followed through.

"Sorry," she said, and meant it. "It's just… All this time, I wasn't actually sure that you even liked me."

The moment the words came out of Nora's mouth, she regretted them. Letting such ignominies slip in front of Ben over the phone, in the quiet, the night crowding in around her, had been one thing. But in person? It left her defenceless, and her defences were her lifeblood.

Ben breathed out hard and fell back on the bed beside her, the mattress bouncing with him. For he was a big guy, in all the best possible ways.

He was quiet for a moment. A long moment.

She risked a glance to find he'd tucked one big, strong arm loosely behind his head. The other rested on top of the covers, which only came to his waist, leaving his stunning torso bare, his profile a study in manly beauty.

To think she'd traced the lines of his ribs with the flat of her hand. Felt his muscles contract under her touch, while he'd tried to stay in control. Followed the trail of dark hair that came together in an arrow leading—

"I *like* my coffee sweet," said Ben, as if he'd worked hard on his answer.

"Hmm? What now?"

Ben tipped his head. "I *like*," he reiterated, "my avocado smashed. My socks to be one hundred per cent cotton."

"Could you be more preppy?"

"You're determined to put a label on this."

Her eyes snapped back into focus to find him looking deep into her eyes. "Labelling things helps me remember where the landmines are buried, and where I've yet to map. It's a thing of mine."

"A thing of mine is that I do not put you in the same category as avocado on toast or cotton-rich socks."

Nora's next breath in stuttered. If Ben noticed, he let her be.

Deep down, she so wanted to be liked. She craved it. Having been told, over and over, that she wasn't enough, or was just too much, she'd learned that being affable, easy-going, helpful, of use—*happy*—made her likeable in a way that she could control.

Unlocking her Sunshine Mode had been like tapping into some magical power. It put her in the driver's seat, no longer at the whim of anyone else's opinion or desire.

Ben, for all his Ben-ness, would be no different. He'd tire of her. Or become distracted by some other shinier, easier thing. And that was okay. It was life.

And so she would do as she always did, and leave while she was ahead. Before she was pushed. His liking her or not, her liking him—or more than liking, as was clearly becoming the case—couldn't and wouldn't play into that decision.

"All that talk of avocado toast has made me hungry," she said. "You hungry? There's a pub across the way. They do a mean steak. Unless you're bushed. And just want to go to bed."

The glint in his eyes gave her ideas. So many ideas.

She rolled her eyes in order to break eye contact, lest she give into those ideas. For, despite all of her fancy self-talk, she was not impervious. Not to him.

Then she smiled her sunshiniest smile, and sing-songed, "Steak it is! Now get the heck out of my bed, big boy, get dressed, and let's go!"

CHAPTER NINE

As Nora pressed through the Shenanigans crowd she instantly wondered if she'd made a huge mistake.

Her plan had been to show the place off—it was infamous for great food and atmosphere far beyond the borders of Fitzroy—and have him meet some of the younger locals. Make him see this was a place a successful guy from London could fit right in.

But as she angled her way through the early-evening crowd she noted the number of people who stopped talking as they looked Ben's way. Maybe they knew who he was. Or maybe they'd figured out sooner than she had that beneath the stuffed-shirt stubbornness lurked the dark charisma of a bit of a bad boy.

Because the stairs. And then the wall. Then the top of the stairs. Then her bed. Rolling around, clothes flying, hands everywhere. All salty, and hot, and reckless. And then there was that thing he did with his—

Nora tripped. Over nothing, bar her own metaphorical tongue.

Ben's hand reached out and captured her elbow, steadying her.

She glanced back. Caught his questioning smile. And even though all that warm, hard male skin was hidden away behind a chambray shirt and dark jeans, spot fires still popped up all over her body.

She spun front in the hopes he might not notice the blood rush to her cheeks, but could still feel him behind her; all big, and broad, cutting a swathe through the place like a hot knife through butter.

Nora breathed out in relief when she caught Sam the bartender's eye as they approached the bar. "Hey, Sam! I heard you aced your uni results. You're killing it."

Sam lit up; her sunshine working its magic.

"By the way, this is Ben. Clancy's grandson."

Sam's eyes lit up. "Clancy was great. My ma was in her book club. We miss her heaps around here."

Nora glanced back to see Ben take the note with a smile. But only a quick one that didn't quite reach his eyes. None of the bottomless warmth and subtle humour that had filled their depths when it had been just the two of them. Alone. In her bed.

Nora, cheeks starting to hurt from fake smiling, said to Sam, "We sure do. I'd love a cider. Ben?"

"Sounds good," said Ben.

"Sam, can we grab a spot for early dinner?"

"Sure. Take the corner booth," said Sam, popping the tops off a couple of ciders before sliding them across the bar.

Nora took a swig as she checked out the corner booth. It was big and secluded. The kind of booth in which you could get away with all kinds of things under cover of near darkness.

"Any other tables available?" Nora asked.

"Nope. Have a couple of groups coming in. All booked up."

"Cool. Cool, cool, cool." When she caught Ben's gaze, she was rewarded with the slow, sexy rise of a single eyebrow that threatened to short-circuit her brain.

"No-o-o-ra?" Misty said, the vowel suggestively elongated.

Groaning inwardly, Nora turned to find Misty slinking up to their little group, and tried desperately to convey with wide eyes and gritted teeth that Misty should please behave. "Misty, you remember Ben, right?"

"Of course. Bennett Hawthorne, back in the flesh."

"Hey, Misty," Ben said, his deep voice creating hot skitters up and down Nora's spine. "How's tricks?"

"Tricks are fine. So, Clancy left you the house. Were you surprised? After what went down between you?"

Nora coughed on her drink.

Ben's arm reached out to slide across Nora's back, giving her a light rub that sent sparks shooting in every which direction. It was followed by a hearty thump. His way of saying thanks so much for bringing him here.

Nora shot him a glance of apology only to find him looking cool, and unfazed, and unutterably handsome. And his hand didn't move. It stayed, his thumb making slow circles over her spine.

"Menus," said Sam handing a pair across the bar.

Misty snapped them up. "Super, I'll join you."

Ben pulled out his phone and paid for the drinks, then he held an arm before him, and the ladies led the way.

An hour, a drink, a steak dinner later, the bar was hopping. And the corner booth was the place to be.

Christos from the fruit shop had pulled up a chair. Maryanne who ran the vintage book shop joined them, along with the twins who worked the coffee machine at Ambrosia. When Janey from the florist realised Ben was the very man who'd helped them renegotiate a brilliant new lease agreement, she threw herself bodily at him and hugged him tight.

So many drinks had been shouted, eventually Nora had to make a move to the ladies' room.

Wanting to get back to Ben—only so she could act as mediator and bodyguard—she peed faster than she'd ever peed in her life. Wiping her clean hands down the sides of her boho skirt as the bathroom had run out of paper towel, she banged into Misty in the dark hall.

"Whoa!" cried Misty. "What's the rush? Your man is doing just fine without you running interference."

Nora scoffed. "He's not my man."

"Honey, if you haven't spent half the night imagining crawling into his lap and nibbling on whatever bare skin you can reach, I'll eat my shoes."

Nora leant against the wall to let a couple of women pass, and said nothing.

"If it helps," Misty added, "he's been watching you as if he's never seen the sun shine so brightly before."

Strange that something could feel really nice but not help a bit. Under cover of semi-darkness Nora heard herself say, "I may have nibbled a little already."

"Atta girl." Misty put up a hand for a high five, which Nora bluntly refused to meet.

She moved to glance round the corner of the

hall, and found Ben surrounded by intrigued locals, all of whom were hoping to find a little spark of Clancy in him. He absorbed their stories, their loss, with grace and kindness. But even from here she could see the tightness around his jaw, the exhaustion creating creases at the corners of his eyes.

And it hit her, he was grieving too. Whether he wanted to admit it or not.

And *that* was her job here, not to nibble on the guy. Not to give the man hidden pieces of herself. Not to find solace in him.

She'd had her fun. Now the real work had to start.

The night air was brisk, but sweet compared with the spate of sludgy, grey days Ben had left behind in London. The streetlights stymied any view of any stars, but managed to create their own kind of whimsy all the same.

There was no denying the feeling of home with a dash of unreal, Nora ambling beside him; her hair, long and loose, caught by the slight breeze, sending tendrils of spun gold floating about her face.

Nora shivered. And without overthinking it, Ben moved closer, put an arm around her shoulder and said, "I like your friends."

She stiffened a moment, shooting him a look of surprise, before allowing it. A pragmatist at heart. "Did you like them as much as you like avocado on toast?" she asked.

His laughter was swept up by the night.

Then, just as they'd found a rhythm, their steps, their breaths in sync, they neared the house. Nora took him by the hand and untwirled herself from his side, let her fingers slip through his, then hastened up the steps to unlock the front door.

"The alarm?" he reminded her, when she sashayed inside the house.

"Ah," said Nora, spinning on one foot, giving him a look that was full of mischief, before backtracking to the door, "the alarm. Sure."

She walked up to the big plant in the corner, moved back a bunch of fronds to reveal a small, dust-covered panel. She wrenched at it till it opened, then said, "Beep-boop-boop-beep."

"Beep-boop-boop-beep?" he repeated.

She turned back to him with a beatific smile, with a definite impish spark. The power of it hit like a smack between the ribs.

Then something came over her face, a kind of soft, breezy calm. It was as if the woman who had grabbed him by the shirtfront and kissed him on the stairs, the woman who'd refused to give up on him, had called him daily to get him here, had been replaced by a bright, airy, translucent version of herself.

And he felt a flicker of discord deep in his gut.

A match to the flicker he'd felt when she'd come back to the table at the pub. Something…off.

"Coffee?" she asked, her tone light as she tossed her keys into a small bowl on the hall table and bounded towards the kitchen. "I have plenty of sugar. Or decaf if you're worried it'll keep you up."

"No, thanks. Thinking I should hit the sack. You?"

Her face half turned. Enough for him to see the colour rise in her cheeks, the heat flare behind the smoky blue, before she extinguished it as patently as if she'd stuck her head in a bucket of water.

"Glass of water for me. Hydration is an excellent cure for jet lag too. Keen?"

"Sure. Why not?" he said as he watched her fuss about in the kitchen, humming beneath her breath like some cartoon princess.

If not for the fact that they had all but torn one another's clothes off a few scant hours before, he might have believed he'd imagined the pull, the gravity, the connection he'd felt across the phone line. That he'd misread the signs.

Or, worse, been played.

Ben ran a hand through his hair. She had no reason to lie to him. It was this house—old ghosts playing tricks with his head. Yet for all that, he couldn't discount what his gut was telling him: for all that he was drawn to her, he didn't really know her.

Perhaps her suggestion that they were finding solace in one another's arms wasn't so far from the truth. Or, in fact, a bad thing. Yet, at the very thought, a wave of exhaustion swept over him, making his eyes feel heavy and his legs a little loose. "Look, I think I'll just—"

"Oh, no." Nora looked up from the sink, neither airy nor translucent. As if the latent energy she'd been keeping in check had spilled free; she practically glowed.

While Ben reeled from the impact, she quickly glanced over her shoulder, towards the back of the house, and said, "Um—look, I'm really sorry, but—"

"Arooo!"

Ben stilled. "What the hell…?"

"Arooo!"

Yep, it was definitely a howl. A howl of desperation and psychic pain.

Nora shot Ben a look before she fled into the darkness towards the back of the house. Towards the God-awful sound. And he heard the sound of the door creaking open. The back door that didn't lock.

"Nora!" he called, moving after her, his hand unerringly finding the hallway light.

A desperate whimper filled the air, followed by Nora's voice, stage-whispering from a room beyond, "Hello. I know. Good boy. Are you okay? Did you get stuck? Poor darling. Down. Yes. Good boy. No, down!"

"Nora?" he bellowed. "What the hell's going on?"

Her murmuring stopped, and she slowly edged around the laundry door. Her face was alight with pure guilt—which, he realised with a flicker of concern, he much preferred to the blank sweetness. A huge, scruffy grey dog pulled against her grip while with all of her might she hugged it between her knees.

"This big galoot knocked a planter over, blocking off the doggy door. So they were *stuck* outside. All afternoon. And this one is afraid of the dark, you see."

"They?" Ben asked, right as, out of the corner of his eye, he spotted a small fluffy dog, with only one eye and a notch taken out of one ear, standing on the kitchen bench. Growling at him.

He leapt back, a hand over his heart, and swore to blue heaven. "What the hell is going on here?"

Nora glanced from the dog wriggling between her legs to the one on the bench. It would have been funny if not for the fact he could practically see her brain trying to come up with a likely story.

"Nora," he said, his tone brooking no argument. "The truth."

He saw her waver. He saw her decide. As if

truth was a thing to be metered out, not cut and dried as it was to him.

"The truth," he reiterated.

"Of course," she said, shaking her head. "This one is Cutie. He's here to befriend Pie. That one's Pie. Pie doesn't like people. Clancy was fostering him when she...when she died."

When Clancy died. And Nora was there, looking after her house, her foster dog, the cooking, the cleaning. Looking after Clancy, while Ben had been going about his life, busy working, arrogantly sure he had a handle on his life, when he hadn't had a clue.

"It's been a whole thing," Nora went on. "And I'm sorry I didn't tell you about them, but I... This is going to sound so stupid, but they are foster dogs, and I was a foster kid, and I've felt like a hypocrite, wanting to send them back."

Ben swore beneath his breath. And took a moment as his heart began to recover from its caveman-about-to-battle-a-sabre-tooth-tiger rate.

There was truth and there was *truth*. And Nora, as was her way, had hidden the small and gifted him the big. More than he'd asked. More than the timing of their relationship deserved. Unless they were more than strange bedfellows after all.

Ben looked to the small offender on Clancy's bench. All battle scars and patchy fur. It stared at him with its one good eye and he felt a strange echo rush through him. As if he was staring down a canine version of himself, the day he'd arrived at this very house.

"Pie, is it?" he murmured, taking a step towards the bench, keeping eye contact with the ball of scruff. "How's tricks, Pie?"

Pie huffed out a long-suffering breath.

"Like that, is it?" Ben asked, his voice gentling all the more as he approached. Then he held out a hand, palm down, a good foot away from the dog's mouth.

"Wait!" cried Nora, shuffling closer with the big dog still stringing between her knees.

Ben curled his fingers and turned his hand over and let it stay there, near the smaller dog's nose. "For?"

"Aren't you allergic? Or, traumatised somehow? Humans might not be so good at telling if someone doesn't really like them, but dogs can."

Ben baulked. "Who doesn't like dogs?"

Nora baulked back. "People. People who live in minimalist apartments. People who wear ridiculously nice clothes they don't want to get dog hair all over. People who say 'no pets' in their lease agreements."

Ah. Now they were getting somewhere. "Did I say that?"

"Ah, yes! Way back at the beginning. In your first email. Don't you remember?"

Ben shook his head. "It is a common rule for renters. Yes?"

"You mean you just threw it in there as an aside?" Nora rolled her eyes. "Jeez, Ben! I've been terrified about you finding out about these two. Now you're telling me it didn't matter?"

"Oh, it matters, Nora," said Ben. "It matters that you hid it from me. I don't appreciate being lied to."

She nibbled at her bottom lip. "Sometimes it's necessary to fudge the truth a little. To stave off hurt feelings. To make your stories a little more exciting. To avoid overdue library fees. But that's not what you mean."

Ben shook his head even though he got that she'd had her mixed-up reasons, reasons that made it hard for him to feel truly aggrieved.

Nora cleared her throat. "Then I'd better tell you that's how I broke the washing machine. Washing the dog blankets. There was so much fur. And maybe a tennis ball caught up in the folds. And a stick. And the old engine couldn't cope."

Ben's gaze shifted from the little dog and back to Nora. To those big blue eyes. And that face. Wide open. So lovely it made his gut clench.

But he knew Nora was feeling bad for having been caught, not having done the deed in the first place. In Ben's world, the difference was everything.

"Anything else?" he asked.

"Probably."

Ben laughed, unable to hold it back even if he'd tried.

Trouble, he thought and not for the first time.

And while that should have sent him to bed, alone, with a big caveat as to how much of himself he'd open up to this foxy, conflicting, singular woman, he moved in, placed his hands on Nora's cheeks, tilted her lovely face to his and kissed her.

It was the only way to be sure that no more fudged truths fell from her lips. For now.

Her mouth opened on a soft sigh of surprise, before one arm, then the other reached up to wrap around his neck as she lifted onto her toes and pressed her body against his as if she'd been waiting for eons to be able to do so again.

It was over before it started as they were joined by a bag of muscle and bone, with a tail like a leather whip, as Cutie jumped to join the embrace.

Nora pulled away laughing, her face flushed, her eyes bright, as she held the dog at bay with gentle shushing. Then, after shooting Ben a quick look of apology and bemusement, she dragged Cutie towards the laundry room.

Pie—who had somehow found a way down off the bench—now stood at Ben's feet. Looking at him. He reached down, slowly, and gave it its own scruff behind the ear.

After a beat, the dog harrumphed, turned, and headed into the laundry room as well.

When she came out, after having fed and locked up the dogs for the night, Ben was leaning back against kitchen bench. Whatever she saw in his face, she stopped, her hands clasped together in front of her.

"We should talk."

"Sounds ominous."

"Quite the opposite," he said, adding a smile. "There's no room in my life for fiction. Or secrets. Covering up is how my clients get themselves into trouble in the first place. And while I'm not prepared to talk about what happened between Clancy and me, suffice it to say it lies down that path."

Nora listened. Her expression was neither Stepford Wife–blank, nor mischief and trouble. It was wary. Considering. And he wondered if he was finally getting a glimpse into a side of her she rarely showed.

Nora in her truth.

Ben pushed away from the bench, not letting the weight of that stop him in his current path. "I live in London. Soon you'll be heading off as well. The one thing bringing us together will be at an end and we'll likely never see one another again. Still, while we are here, together, I'd like to spend time with you. And I'd like to know how you feel about that."

Ben didn't move as he waited for her answer. For a breath, or three, while thoughts too fast to discern raged and stormed behind her eyes, he believed it might be a no.

"Temporary," she eventually said. "With the end in sight. Agreed upon. By the both of us."

He nodded.

"One condition," she said, her voice more strident now. "So long as I'm here, you continue helping out the locals with some financial advice."

Ben's right eye twitched. "Behind that sweet face of yours is the mind of a mercenary."

Her eyes narrowed.

"Fine," he said. "Then I have my own addendum. You stay as long as I need help sorting out Clancy's things." He looked around, felt the buzz of the past biting him on the back of the neck. "Truth is, I'm finding the idea a tad...overwhelming."

Her narrowed eyes softened, before filling with purpose. A smile nudged up a corner of her sweet mouth.

Say yes, his inner voice begged, *so I can kiss that spot as soon as humanly possible.*

"Deal," she said, then held out her hand.

He took it, using it to tug her to him, before lifting her off her feet and into his arms. Kissing her till the world outside their door began to melt away.

"Where are you taking me?" Nora asked as he began to walk her down the hall.

"Your bed," he said. "Mine's too small for the plans I have."

"Promises, promises," she said, pulling back, to hold a hand to his cheek, her gaze following, before it landed back on his.

No guile therein. No faux innocence. No blank sweetness. No secrets. No lies.

Just Nora. The Nora he'd crossed oceans to find.

At the top of the stairs, he shoved her bedroom door open with a foot, and tossed her onto the bed. Both of them laughing. And he knew; if she could forgive him for not being there in what had to have been some of her darkest days, he could forgive her for hiding the truth about the dogs.

In the grand scheme of things, their ledger wasn't even close to even.

CHAPTER TEN

THE NEXT DAY, after he'd spent a couple of hours going over Damon's updates on the work done on the Metropolis account in his absence, making note as to where the team might put more eyes, Ben stood outside the sitting room, gaze pinging off the walls of books, overstuffed couches, floor rugs, throw cushions, baskets of dried flowers, knick-knacks on every surface, trying not to settle on any memories in particular lest they drown him.

"I've set up a few bags and boxes in the entrance, labelled donate, gift, sell, keep." Nora pulled up beside him, hands rubbing together, her voice bright, excited. "So, you want to start in here?"

Ben turned to her, slid an arm around her waist, pulled her close. "I'd rather start here," he growled. And then he kissed her.

Laughing against his mouth, she started to pull back, before her body stilled, softened, and rolled against his and she kissed him like a woman drowning.

And soon Ben was lost in far better memories—the taste of her skin, the way her body moved, lithe and fearless, the sounds she made as she fell apart in his arms.

"No," she said, slapping him on the chest. "Not now. Later. Consider it a reward for a job well done."

"Fine. How about you move your stuff first so it doesn't get mixed up?"

"My stuff is all upstairs. Fits into a single suitcase and a small backpack."

"Seriously?"

"Mmm-hmm. Can't be footloose and fancy-free if you're weighed down with baggage." She ran a thumb over the tattoo on her arm, as if it was some kind of touchstone. And proffered him one of her gentle smiles—the light, easy, unassuming type. The one that made him feel as though if he reached out for her, she wouldn't actually be there.

But if he was going to get through this today, and the next, he needed the real thing—the raw, dark, slippery smile he'd only ever seen her offer him.

"Should I be worried?" he asked. "Are you on the lam? Ready for a quick getaway? If you try to vamoose before I get through this, I will find you and bring you back."

At that she laughed, the sound low yet enormously compelling. "I'm not going anywhere." A shadow passed over her eyes. Then she shrugged. "I had to pack fast, a lot, as a kid. Circumstances tended to change quickly."

"A skill you might not have picked up otherwise," he said, happy to shift focus from himself for a moment. Or for ever.

"Correct! I also taught myself how to cook, knowing it would mean I'd always get fed."

"Brilliant. What else?"

"I can shape-shift to fit into different situations—loud, wholesome, alpha, nerdy. It really helps put different clients at ease."

That, Ben thought, a frisson of edginess creeping back in, that was the feeling he'd had the night before when he'd all but seen the masks slip into place. Cheeky and honest and brave. Sweet and sparkly and inoffensive. She was a chameleon.

Everyone was to some degree; Nora, perhaps, more than most. So long as that was all it was. Not that she was faking everything.

"Now," she said, before the silence grew awkward. "Let's do this!"

She padded into the sitting room, and stood in the middle, arms outstretched. All lanky legs and mismatched clothes. She looked so right, so part of the room, Ben's chest tightened.

Or maybe it was the fact that he'd delayed

enough. He had to go in there. And clean up Clancy's mess.

"You could rent the house fully furnished. Or there's a local domestic violence shelter I've done some pro bono work for who would love anything you could give them. How about we focus on the keepsakes first? Start small. Tell me, what do you remember most about this room?"

Ben's throat began to tighten, his mouth filling with the sharp tang of stale anger. He'd just come back from having drinks at the local pub with a couple of old school mates, when he'd found Clancy in this room. It had been summer, the fire grate empty. The room lit by a single lamp. She'd been holding a piece of paper. Tears pouring down her cheeks.

But when she'd looked up, he'd not seen sorrow in Clancy's eyes, he'd seen dread.

"Ben?" Nora weaved her way back to him.

When he didn't respond, his throat now thick with anger and regret, she reached out, curled her fingers into his.

"If I'm going too fast, or being too chipper, let me know," she said. "I told you, I'm a shape-shifter extraordinaire. Whoever you need for me to be, I can be."

Whoever he needed her to be.

The irony was suddenly so bitter he could taste it in the back of his throat.

Ben yanked his hand away. "I've got to go."

"Oh?" She blinked, confused. "Okay. Where?"

"Out." Away from here. Away from her.

He could feel her need to help, to fix, as if it were a physical thing. But he also felt as if he might stop breathing if he didn't get some air. If he didn't get out of that damn house.

He mumbled something about being back soon, and burst out of the room, out of the unlocked front door, and down the street, not even caring which direction he was going.

Nora sat staring out of the window from her upstairs bedroom. It was late afternoon and she'd heard nothing from Ben for hours.

She'd tried calling him with a bland excuse at the ready, only to track his ringtone—classic, no pop song for him—to the spare room. His suitcase sat neatly against the wall. Nothing unpacked. As if he didn't want to leave an impression on the place. She knew that move intimately, and it did not bode well.

He'd said he wasn't ready to talk about Clancy, but it had become clear there was some crack inside where that was concerned; unhealed, buffed over. Even now—if the look on his face was anything to go by—he was out there, in pain.

When she realised she was rubbing the heel of her palm over her ribs, right over her heart, in fact, Nora whipped her hand away.

This wasn't empathy she was feeling. It was something else entirely.

Despite his pretty words, his bold suggestion they "spend time together" until their job here was done, and despite her belief in that moment that she was fine with that, she'd been hasty.

She liked the man. More than avocado on toast. More than any man she'd ever known. She liked his smile, his laugh. She liked his self-awareness, his arrogance, his self-containment, his focus. She liked the way he looked at her, the way he kissed her, the way he never baulked whenever she was accidentally vulnerable.

What she didn't like was that, despite all that, he had the ability to hurt her without meaning to, or wanting to, just like the rest of them.

Either way she couldn't sit around waiting for him to come back. It was driving her nuts.

Padding down the stairs, she found Pie sitting at the front door, his little nose twitching as he stared at the patch of sunshine slicing through the mail slot. Turned out she wasn't the only one waiting for Ben to return.

Her heart—unguarded, unprepared—gave a twitch. Then a thump. And didn't quite go back to the same spot it had been before.

Muttering under her breath about toughening up, for Pete's sake, about keeping a clear head and staying the course, she shucked her feet into a pair of sandals, instructed both dogs to stay put, and headed out of the door.

Across the road, Misty was sitting on her stoop, blowing bubbles, as if that might bring in custom. Misty lifted her chin in greeting. "You guys disappeared like old smoke last night. Was sure I wouldn't see either of you for days."

"Funny. On that note, you seen Ben, by any chance?"

"Why?"

"He just… He went out in a bit of a hurry. And I want to make sure he isn't…lost, or something."

"Lost? A man that huge can't get lost." Misty stopped, mid bubble blow, her eyes dancing over Nora's face. "Why did he leave in a bit of a hurry?"

"Ah… He's starting the clean-up of Clancy's stuff today. I'm helping."

"He's down with that?"

"Me helping?"

"Going through Clancy's stuff."

"I…hadn't asked." Nora remembered again the look on his face just before he'd left, and her heart squeezed in her chest. "It can't be fun, for anyone, but I truly believe this whole process will be good for him. Cathartic."

"Don't know about that. Some people like to reminisce. Others like to burn the past to the ground. You know what's truly cathartic? Those glowing cheeks of yours, the lopsided stride, the hickey on your neck."

Nora's hand went straight to the spot on her neck that Ben particularly liked to nibble.

Then Misty's eyes narrowed. "Looks like the man knows how to lead. Are you letting him do that? Or are you spreading your sunshine all over the place and hoping he'll do as he's told?"

Nora blinked. Gawped. Struggled to find an apt response.

Misty shook her head. "You're a smart cookie, Nora, and ridiculously compassionate. But you're a nuffy when it comes to the big stuff."

Nora crossed her arms. Then uncrossed them, not wanting to appear defensive. Or feel that way, to be honest. "What big stuff?"

"Ben Hawthorne is a big, important guy. He sorts out multinational conglomerates, business empires, small countries. He did not come all the way over here to sort out his grandmother's dress closet."

Misty waited, as if Nora might suddenly click her fingers and say, *I get it.* But she did not. Could not. Would not. Forcing Misty to shout, "Honey bun, the man came home for *you.*"

Nora waited for the bluster and fluster of outrage to come over her. Instead, Misty's words uncurled beneath her defences, like a cat waking up and stretching after a long, luxurious nap in the sun.

"So take care," said Misty, "and give the man some credit, that's all I'm saying. Drinks tomorrow?"

Nora gave her a thumbs up before she turned and walked back towards home. Clancy's home. *Ben's* home. Not hers. She'd been a tenant, but now was merely a guest, at the mercy of Ben's pleasure. His choice, his decision, his lead.

Add the feelings she was feeling for the guy, feelings swirling through her, bumping into one another, making her feel hot, and flustered and nauseous, and she hadn't realised how little control she had over the whole situation until that moment.

Misty might have been right about some things, but she was wrong about the sunshine. Nora had thought she was deep in Sunshine Mode, but she'd been skirting the edges, letting Ben's ease, and strength, drag her towards the centre.

If she was going to get through the next couple of weeks in one piece, it was time to ramp things up.

Ben walked for hours, past new stores and old pubs, in search of air, space, and perspective. Or, at a pinch, a teleportation device that could take him back to London, a month or two before, when his life had been logical and straightforward and steady.

Before Clancy had died. Before he'd ever heard of *The Girl Upstairs*.

Hell, maybe he'd go back further, a couple of years even, to before he'd found Clancy reading the letter over the empty fire grate in the sitting room. The letter telling her that Ben's birth mother had died.

Ben's birth mother who, as it had turned out, had also been Clancy's daughter.

Aida.

Aida, who'd left Ben on Clancy's doorstep when he was five years old. Aida, whom Clancy had told if she walked away she'd never be allowed to return. Aida, who'd been living in the world, for twenty-something years, without Ben's knowledge.

All of which he'd only discovered a week after Aida had died.

Clancy had lied to him. Outright. For years. Calling him her "adopted grandson", which, she'd later argued, was mostly true. The grandmother part, not the adopted part. As if that justified what she'd done.

She'd taken from him the chance to meet his mother. Even when he was a grown man, she'd kept it from him. She'd been so stubborn and sure of herself.

By the time Ben finished walking, the sun had begun to set and the early evening chill started to cut through his clothes. The streetlamps created pools of golden light up and down the block and the house—his grandmother's house—looked down at him, all but daring him to make a decision already.

Sell me. Rent me. Move in. Give me away. Burn me to the ground. Walk away and never look back.

The only decision Ben made was to go inside, as Nora would be there, and that was as far as he could think.

Music played softly from Clancy's old radio in the kitchen. The dogs lay splayed out on a blanket in the entrance—the little one's tail wagged as it saw him, the big one snored through.

Nora sat curled up on the big, soft couch in the sitting room; a blanket wrapped about her shoulders, a book in her lap. The fire flickering behind the grate sent long shadows about the room, making her skin look warm to the touch.

Even at this distance he could feel her in the air. As if she mucked with his perspective on a cellular level. Despite his assurances, to her and himself, there was no way he was getting out of this thing unscathed. The only part of the story left untold was whether it would be his doing, or hers.

He must have made a sound as she spun on the chair and looked up, those big blue eyes of hers luminous in the low light, and shadowed with worry. For him. The guy people came to when they were in trouble. It was a hell of a thing.

"Hey," she said, her voice soft, rough from under-use. Then she closed her book gently, using her finger as a bookmark. "Want a cuppa?"

"No. Thank you. I'm good. I grabbed something when I was out."

She uncurled her legs, as if to make room for him. He moved into the room, for the first time in over two years. And he sat. The ancient springs tilted them both towards the centre. Towards one another.

Smiling still, all sweetness and light, she held up her book. *"Jane Eyre."*

"Ah."

"Have you read it?"

"I have, actually. A long time ago. Rite of passage, growing up here. All a bit dramatic for my taste."

Nora laughed, the sound simplifying everything and creating a quickening inside him, all at once. "I know, right? But Clancy adored it. Was it the drama, or the house, or was there a tragic love affair in her past; a Rochester of her own?"

He was aware Nora was making conversation in order to alleviate whatever tension had sent him running in the first place, but she had no idea she'd just stumbled over the exact reason he'd wanted to be anywhere but here.

Clancy. Love. Affairs. Family. The lies binding them together.

Nora moved, the blanket dropping away to reveal a loose T-shirt hanging off one shoulder. He knew how fast he could lose himself in that soft warmth of her neck. How it would make all of the noise in his head disappear.

Wanting her because he wanted her was biology. Using her to block out the ghosts in his head was an ass move. He sat forward instead, letting his head fall into his hands.

"Dammit," she said, her voice velvet soft, a little edgy. "I was trying so hard not to push. But it's what I do. You don't have to tell me anything. Or do any of the things I suggest. I have thick skin, Ben, so please, don't be afraid to tell me to shut up. Or back off. Or leave."

"Don't," Ben said, the word busting out of him. "Don't...ask?"

"Don't leave. Not yet."

He heard Nora's sharp intake of breath beside him, before she eventually whispered, "I'm right here."

Then she reached out, her hand landing on his knee, in nothing but comfort. But the scent of her, the warmth, the sincerity, the complexity, knocked about the empty spaces inside him. Begging to be let in. To fill him up. To help him forget.

He clenched his jaw hard enough he heard a crack.

"If you're keen on sticking with the strong, silent thing," she said, "more power to you. You wear it well. But the best thing about me is that I'm nothing to you. A firefly flittering past in the night. Whatever you tell me goes with me. If that helps at all."

Ben lifted his head from the cage of his hands and turned her way.

She was so still. So calm. Her focus, complete. The power of it, of her, when she wasn't putting on a show, when she was simply being, was staggering. And she had no idea.

"You are not nothing, Nora."

Her recoil was infinitesimal, but he felt it. "I'm sorry?"

"You, Nora Letterman, are not nothing."

Her eyes sparked with defiance. "*That's* not what I meant. Of course, I'm not *nothing*. I'm amazing! What I meant to say was, in the grand scheme of things, I'm unimportant to you."

Ben slowly sat up straight. "I'm not sure where you're getting your news, Nora, but you are *not* nothing, and you are not unimportant to me. If you were, you would not be sitting here, beside me, in Clancy's house, with your hand on my knee."

She pulled her hand away as if burnt.

He caught it; brought it back to his side of the

couch. Cupped both of his larger hands around hers. Felt her fingers curl into his palm.

She shook her head, but didn't pull away. "Everything's coming out wrong. My point is, none of this is meant to be about me. This, me being here, sticking around, this is all about you. Helping you."

For a long fraught moment her eyes remained stuck on his. He felt as if he were falling into her, till he could feel all of her parts—the fire and smarts and savvy and insecurity, the sensitivity and the blinders, the damage and the heart.

Eventually, she said, "I'm sorry, but I'm struggling here. You won't tell me what happened between you and Clancy, but you want me to trust that you're a good guy in all this, even though Clancy is...*was* one of the loves of my life. You want to stay, to help, but now you don't want that? What is it you want from me, Ben?"

"Nora, just give me a minute."

After a moment, Nora gently tugged her hand free and tucked it back, safe, into the folds of her blanket and said, "Okay."

Ben coughed out a humourless laugh. He didn't do this—talk, share, self-examine. But somehow this complicated creature had unravelled him without even trying. Forced him to think about things he'd kept locked up for years. Clancy, his mother, his loss, on both counts. Till the ropes that held him together felt frayed, and untethered, unrecognisable.

He had to let some of it out or he'd explode. Could he tell her about Clancy? About the falling out, or the feeling he had as to why Clancy had taken on a tenant for the first time in her life, his suspicion that she'd known she was sick a long time before she let on?

No. It would break Nora's heart. And he knew her enough to know there was a very good chance she'd shoot the messenger. Perhaps he could lead her there, gently. Help her figure it out on her own. It wasn't a lie. He was protecting her.

And if that wasn't the most ironic moment of his entire life, he wasn't sure what was.

He glanced across, found the fire playing over her hair, her face, her eyes, like a rainbow caused by sunlight slicing through a crystal. Her eyes were bright, restive. If he felt laid bare, it was clear she did too.

He held her gaze as he said, "It's been a rough few weeks."

"Yep."

"But through it all, you've been the lighthouse in the storm. A warm voice at the end of some bitterly cold days. The cream in my coffee."

She swallowed. "And there I was thinking I was a pain in your ass."

"That too." A smile settled on his mouth. She did that. It was a gift. He bumped her knee with his, then left it there. "If you really want to help me, Nora, I don't need advice, or a nudge, or to be pushed. I can do what needs to be done. If you really want to help, all I need is for you to be you."

She pressed her knee more fully against his, and said, "That might just be the most spectacularly lovely thing anyone has ever said to me." Her brow furrowed before smoothing. "And that's not me being cute, or sassy, or…whatever. I mean it."

He smiled.

She smiled.

Then her blanket slipped again, tugging her top with it so he got an eyeful of warm creamy shoulder, a whole lot of décolletage and the truth colouring what *else* he wanted from her twisted all over again.

Ben pressed his hands to his knees and stood. "With that," he said on the back of an old-man groan, "I'm going to head to bed early tonight. I am officially dead on my feet."

Nora wrapped the blanket tighter around herself as she stood, her bare feet curling into the rug, the glowing embers creating dips and shadows on her lovely face. "Sure. Good plan. Smart. I'll head up too. Alone. To my room. Keep the place quiet for you. Goodnight, Ben."

"Goodnight, Nora."

With that she ducked out of the room, her voice

calling softly for the dogs to follow. Which they did, the little one giving Ben a forlorn glance, almost as if it was disappointed in him for not following as well.

I hear ya, buddy, he thought. Then he trudged down the hall to his old room, running both hands over his face as if trying to make the skin fit.

He nudged off his shoes, tugged his jumper over the back of his head, ready to fall on top of the bed and sleep for a year. Then, when he turned on the bedside lamp, he saw a book on the side table.

A copy of *Jane Eyre*, sporting a Post-it note reading, *Read me!* with a little picture of Alice in Wonderland sketched into the corner.

He recognised it instantly as Clancy's copy. The spine faded, pages all but falling apart. He opened the book to find it soft, well-read, dog-eared, with notes in the margin, in Clancy's tiny handwriting; exclamation marks, smiley faces, sighs. A big circle around the first mention of Thornfield Hall.

He could picture the book on side tables, in Clancy's gnarled hands, face down on the hall table. Could feel Clancy's love for high drama, for romance, for her friends, for this house, and for him, as patent as if she were right beside him.

With no plan in mind, Ben headed back out into the hall and through the kitchen to find

Nora at the bottom of the stairs, the blanket still wrapped around her shoulders. One foot was on the floor, the other crooked, as if she was heading down and not up.

Her eyes were huge, luminous in the low light as she whispered, "The book."

Ben held it up.

Her sweet face fell. "Of course, I put it there *before* you said all you said about not wanting my brand of help." She let her hovering foot fall to the floor beside the other one. "But I still feel like a goose. I'm so sorry."

Ben took another step her way. "You have nothing to apologise for."

"I'm pushy."

"You're wonderful. And I'm a cranky bastard. And you're wonderful."

Her mouth fell open in a half-smile. "You might have mentioned that already."

"Bears mentioning twice."

Her throat worked. Her eyes were dark and beguiling. A tug of war being fought behind their depths. When they caught on his, they captured him whole.

"Ben, can I…?" She took a step his way, her hand trailing over the wallpaper. "Can I ask you something? Just one small thing. Something Misty said today—"

"What's that?"

"Actually, forget it."

Ben ambled several slow steps closer, his blood hastening in his veins at the way she watched him. His breaths deepening as he neared. "Nora, not all that many minutes ago I heard myself call you the cream in my coffee like some spotty seventeen-year-old writing bad song lyrics in his bedroom. There is nothing you can say that will top that."

She laughed, the sound husky and raw. "Don't be so sure. Misty suggested today that the reason you've yet to do any of the things I thought you came here to do is that you didn't come back here for Clancy's sake. That you actually came back here for me."

Her eyes fluttered, full of tenderness and doubt. The readiness to be shot down. The complete lack of faith in her own drawing power.

The people in her past, who'd had the chance to know her, to love her, but instead made her feel so unworthy, deserved to be quartered.

Clancy had given him *that* at least. Safety, laughter, and confidence, and the assuredness that whatever he wanted to do with his life, it was his for the taking.

He slowed to a stop. Maybe he couldn't give her the dirty truth, but he could give her this. "You know how little I wanted to be here."

Her nostrils flared, ever so slightly.

"You know I'd have let the place sit, untouched, unwatched, for who knows how long, before I found the wherewithal to deal with it. So then, you must know, the only reason I'm here, now, at all, is because of you."

Nora's eyes were now huge in the half-light. "Ben—"

Ben stepped into her space, reached out, trapping her cheek in his palm.

She leaned into it, her eyes dropping half closed, her brow furrowing, before she seemed to gather herself, lifting her face free from his touch.

"Just… The reason I asked… I can't…"

"I know," he said, his voice gentle. He didn't want to spook her. He wanted to kiss her, and hold her, and exalt her.

"It's not you. You're gorgeous. And successful. And so sure of yourself. While I'm… I'm stronger than I'm sounding right now. But it's taken work to get here. I know I'm not nothing. I do. But I *have* nothing to offer. Apart from this. Being here. Helping you find a way back to Clancy."

Ben reached out for her hand, turned it over so he could see her tattoo. Ran his thumb over the words: *Footloose and fancy-free.*

She believed it too. She'd have to, in order to engrave it into her skin. Problem was, seeing her curled up on the couch, by the fire, book in hand, all rugged up in a soft blanket, dogs at her feet, to Ben she'd looked…

She'd looked like home.

Ben tossed the book onto the nearby hall table.

When he looked back at her, the blanket was falling from her shoulders as she was all but vibrating.

"So, you think I'm gorgeous, do you?"

She rolled her eyes. "I don't become pen pals with just anyone, you know. There's gotta be something in it for me."

"Stop your sweet nothings," he murmured, moving closer. "I might get ideas."

Her hand lifted to rest against his chest. Right over the now thunderous beat of his heart. She was close enough he could happily have drowned in the clean tangy sweetness of her scent. In the silken fall of her hair.

Her eyes lifted heavily to his. Drugged with heat. Need.

"So we're clear. It can't mean anything," she said with a half-hearted press of her hand.

Too late, thought Ben. *It already does.*

He kissed her and she threw herself into his arms. Bodily. Up on her tiptoes, her hands flung around his neck. Her eyes slammed closed and she kissed him back.

He felt the shudder of her breath. As if she'd heard the words he'd not been able to say and they'd loosened all kinds of things inside her. As if she needed him to hold her together, just as she'd been holding him together.

Bending, he slid an arm behind her knees and swept her off her feet, literally, and carried her up the stairs to her tower.

When he slid her gently, preciously, to the floor, she pushed him back onto her bed.

The old mattress bounced and shifted beneath his weight as Nora crawled on her knees towards him.

He let her think she was in control, till she was over the top of him, her hair sweeping the pillow beside him. Then with a growl he flipped her over, catching her laughter with a kiss that sent bursts of something that felt a hell of a lot like pure and simple joy right through him.

And then, after a day of trying to find something, an answer, a path, a plan, he gave up, gave in, and lost himself in her, all night long.

Nora was mindful to remember herself as they continued making their way through the house. Tidying. Cataloguing. Bagging. Stopping if Ben looked as if he might implode, such as when they happened upon Clancy's well-thumbed collection of *Men's Health* magazines. Or when Nora had found a box of cookbooks in the back of the pantry.

Nora started putting out feelers as to where she might end up next. And made sure to spend decent time on finalising her local client work, and posted plenty on her own Instagram page—fun, friendly shots for the Pizza Place, dark, moody, come-get-me vibes for Shenanigans, a most adorable picture of Ben nose to nose with Pie while tagging Playful Paws Puppy Rescue. Because how could she not?

And while, in that one inexplicably lovely moment, Ben had said "all I need is for you to be you," she knew, in her heart of hearts, what they both needed was closure.

So Nora told stories from the last couple of years, trying, gently, to fill in the blanks, to build a bridge back to wherever things had fallen apart between Ben and his adopted grandmother.

In an immensely satisfying move, Ben started telling stories of his own. First there was the calculator he'd found on her bookshelves. He told her how he'd loved the thing so much he used to sleep with it at night. Then there was the fire poker with the missing tip. A fight between Luke Skywalker—Ben—and the Emperor—Clancy— was to blame for that one.

Then there was the subtle easing of his furrowed brow. The way he whistled when making their morning coffees while she buttered their toast. He even spent one whole day in his striped flannelette pyjamas. Man, he looked fine in those things; especially when he ditched the top and padded around barefoot in only the pants.

There was also the lack of hesitation in taking her hand and curling her in for a kiss any time they ended up in the same space for longer than a minute. The way he lingered when kissing the top of her head as he passed her in the kitchen, his arm slung around her shoulder, almost as if he were breathing her in.

A small part of her wondered if it all had more to do with her than the house, but there was no point in going down that path.

When night fell, they often ate in, Nora cooking, as she was good at it and loved the way he hummed when he ate the things she made. Ben, on the other hand, was no cook. "Like grandmother, like grandson," she'd said, to which he'd smiled a little tightly. But it was still nice to discover he wasn't brilliant at everything.

And while every day that Nora stayed was another day on the wrong side of leaving, every day also added more strands to the web from which she'd have to disentangle herself when she eventually did go.

She consoled herself with the fact that the memories she was making, and tucking carefully away, were the kind that would keep her warm for a long, long time.

CHAPTER ELEVEN

A KNOCK SOUNDED at the front door.

Nora looked up from her spot at her laptop by the window to find rain creating rivulets down the window. Huh, it was the first time she remembered seeing rain in weeks.

Ben—asleep and snoring on her bed, arms akimbo, big feet poking out the ends, which had made her inordinately happy for some bizarre reason she had no plan on going into—didn't stir.

Another knock, and what sounded like a "Yoo-hoo!" floating up from downstairs, had Nora leaping from her chair, wrapping a cardigan around her shoulders, and padding down the stairs, Cutie and Pie in tow.

The dogs disappeared into the back of the house—Pie in search of a hidey hole, Cutie in cahoots with Pie—while Nora found a cacophony of older women piling into the foyer. Umbrellas dripping, shaking water droplets all over the floor, they forced Nora back up the stairs.

"Uh…ladies?" Nora said, gripping the railing.

Phyllis—the holder of the spare key, and Clancy's oldest friend, as well as being the doctor who'd been with Nora during Clancy's last days—gave Nora an apologetic smile. "Sorry, love, you weren't answering the door. And there was really no stopping them."

Beryl gave Nora a mutinous glare. "It was Clancy's turn, you see."

"So here we are!" Janet added, waving a book and a bottle of wine.

Sylvia followed. Then Carol. Misty came last, shut the door behind her and shooed everyone deeper into the house.

"Widows' Book Club," Nora realised.

"Yup," said Misty. "Do you still have that bottle of Scotch Clancy opened last time we were here?"

Nora muttered, "A heads up might have been nice."

Misty shrugged, rubbed her hands together, and grinned. "Where's your dastardly landlord?"

It took all of Nora's powers not to glance towards the stairs, where she'd left Ben, face down, naked atop her sheets.

"You okay, honey?" asked Beryl. "You look a little flushed."

"I'm fine. Just great." She angled herself behind the noisy group and hustled them into the sitting room, a couple already sitting on the couch on which she and Ben, just the night before, had—

The women stopped as one, eyes lifting, as if sensing a shimmer in the air, a rush of testosterone flowing through the house, just before Ben's heavy footsteps sounded on the stairs.

"Nora? I thought I heard—" Ben walked into the entrance to the sitting room still tugging his moss-coloured Henley T over his jeans.

"Oh, if it isn't little Ben Hawthorne!" said Phyllis, breaking the loaded silence, her arms stretched out as if for a hug. "They said you were back but I didn't believe it!"

Ben—whether by way of politeness, or habit, or instinct—held out his arms and gathered her in. "Hey, Dr Rand."

Over the top of the doctor's head, Ben's gaze caught on Nora, eyebrows lifting at the situation in which he found himself. Nora simply shrugged. Not enough fairy dust in the world to help him now.

"That man ain't little by any stretch of the imagination," a dismembered voice whispered somewhere behind Nora.

"I hear that," murmured another.

"Who is he?" asked the whisperer.

"Clancy's grandson."

"Oh. I thought they'd fallen out after he found out she was—"

"That's the one."

"Ladies!" said Phyllis, making Nora jump as her ears had been so attuned to the whispers behind her. She'd told herself Ben and Clancy's past was none of her business. But clearly her curiosity was still piqued.

One arm still around Ben's waist, Phyllis said, "Everyone, this is Ben, Clancy's grandson." With that she did introductions all round, finishing with Nora. "Nora, you know Ben? Of course, you must. You're staying here. And he's staying here."

"Um, yep."

Phyllis's eyes opened a fraction wider before glancing towards the stairs. "And... I think it's time we eat?"

Food. If anything was to distract a room full of octogenarian widow book-clubbers from possible sexual intrigue, it was food.

"Settle in. Leave it to me," said Nora, most glad to slip out of the room, with all the unspoken questions hanging over her.

"I'll help," a deep voice rumbled behind her.

She made it into the kitchen before she turned to find Ben standing before her. The top buttons of his Henley were undone, a shadow of dark hair peeking out of the top. Her favourite jeans of his moulded to his strong legs. His feet were bare.

"Hi," she said, her voice barely more than a breath.

"We have visitors."

"The Widows' Book Club. It's Clancy's turn to host."

"Of course it is." His face creased into a long, slow smile, still soft with sleep. With stubble covering his jaw he looked good. He looked happy.

"Teacups!" she said, her voice cracking. "Trays. Do you remember where Clancy kept the—?"

She turned to find Ben with a pair of Wedgwood platters in hand.

"It's all right with you if they stay for a bit?"

"Of course," he said, moving to kiss her, lightly, as he slid a hand under the centre of the tray of cookies she was holding and took it out of her hands. "I'll take this in before they start eating the furniture. I've come to like that sofa and would hate to see it disappear."

The flush flowing through her turned her up to eleven, even as he left her alone in the kitchen.

By the time she collected herself, and enough plates and napkins for the group, Ben had settled into the single armchair in front of the fire.

Nora perched on the edge of the sofa near the entrance, as glasses and cups were raised to Clancy. Then the Widows' Book Club moved on to talking about the books they'd read: everything from self-help, to horror, to young adult romance.

Before long, the women began to creak and groan and rearrange themselves in their chairs, and start muttering about heading home, making her wonder if they'd come for tea and cake and books, or if they'd come to check out little Ben Hawthorne.

Nora, with Ben's okay, told them to raid Clancy's bookshelves, to take as many as they liked.

Phyllis gave her a hug on the way out. "Again, apologies. Lovely to see you looking so well though, love."

Nora felt the tears burning the backs of her eyes all too late. "Thank you."

"Bennett," Janet said, her voice carrying. "Your falling out was the one great regret of Clancy's life. Well, that and losing Gerald, of course."

"Thank goodness for Nora," said Beryl. "Gave your grandmother such joy in the last couple of years. A distraction from her broken heart."

Nora glanced back to find Ben seemed to have developed a tic in his cheek muscle. He murmured something conciliatory, but Nora missed the details as Misty stepped in her path.

"Hey."

"Hey."

"Nice book club."

"Thanks?"

"Shall I stay and help clean up? Or do you have plans for the leftover whipped cream?" Misty tipped her head sideways, in Ben's direction.

Nora held the front door open wide. "There was no whipped cream."

"Check again," said Misty, bringing a tube out of her bag and forcing Nora to take it.

Nora whipped the whipped cream behind her back as they turned to find Ben in the arch of the sitting room, arms crossed, big body holding up the wall.

"Being good, Hawthorne?" Misty asked.

Ben grinned. Nora swooned. Misty turned to Nora with a grin, blew her a kiss and was gone.

Nora slowly shut the door behind her, then turned, leant back on the wood, closed her eyes, and breathed out. She opened one eye, then the next, to find Ben still leaning in the doorway to the sitting room. Looking at her in a way she hadn't seen before.

As if he were seeing her for the first time.

"They're lovely," she said, "but, gosh, they're a whirlwind."

"You held them hostage with muffins."

"I did not. You're making me sound like Little Red Riding Hood."

He clicked his fingers at her as he followed her into the kitchen. "That's exactly it. You head off into the woods, muffins in tow, looking after everyone—the widows, the local shopkeepers, Misty. Does it occur to them that you might need someone to bring muffins to you once in a while?"

"Why would I need muffins when I'm perfectly capable of making my own?" said Nora, wondering how they'd suddenly become so caught up on muffins.

Ben plucked a tea towel from the bench and tugged it through his fingers, again and again. "You're missing the point."

"Which is?"

Ben paused, as if considering whether or not to go on. Whatever he saw in her face decided it for him. "You wanted to help me make peace with Clancy. I want to make sure, when you leave, you don't let the next lot take advantage of you."

Nora shot Ben a look. "Excuse me?"

Ben ran a hand over his face. "I'm going about this all wrong. It's just, watching the dynamic in that room, watching you with Clancy's friends, I wondered, and not for the first time, if Clancy treated you the same way."

Nora coughed out a breath. Then, trying really hard to tap into her well of sunshine, she came up empty. Which meant the only place to turn was Survival Mode.

"If I'm Little Red Riding Hood, surely Clancy was the sweet old grandmother. So that only leaves the big bad wolf."

"Come on, Nora. Clancy was no sweet old grandmother."

Ben was right. Clancy was mad and obstinate and opinionated, but she balanced that out with the ferocity of her support. *But what if...?* Nora suddenly thought. *What might make her take that support away?*

"Why didn't she tell you she was sick?"

Ben breathed out hard through his nose.

"Because you didn't call her, right?"

"It was her turn to call me."

"That's your excuse. It was her turn? Who takes turns calling family? If she missed a call, why didn't you reach out?"

"You don't think I've asked myself the same thing every damn day since?"

As Ben's words echoed in the kitchen, Nora's ire dropped a good ten degrees.

This was *Ben*. Lovely Ben. Measured Ben. The man she… She trusted, and respected, and liked a hell of a lot. Like-liked. Was *like-like-liked* a thing? It should be.

"How did this go from muffins to a battle?" she asked.

Ben gave her a measured look, and said, "Clancy. That's how."

"I know you guys had issues, but Clancy was good to me. She didn't take advantage of me. We found one another at the perfect time in our lives and I'd not change a single second of it. Not even those final weeks."

"Do you have any idea how sweet you are?" said Ben, turning to face her.

"Pfft. I'm not sweet. I'm tough. I'm smart. I

choose my actions. I choose my responses. I'm in charge."

He tossed the tea towel to the bench and held out both hands as if about to hold her by the upper arms, but instead he hovered, just out of reach. "Why didn't you get the alarm on the house sorted?"

"What does that—?"

"The alarm. When I asked you to send Damon details of the alarm company so we could get it connected, why did you resist?"

"Because it was unnecessary. I was fine!"

"I've done a lot of walking since I've been back and this area is riddled with graffiti. I've seen baggies beside bins in the park. Sirens whiz by three times a night."

"That's life in the big city."

"The back door doesn't lock properly."

"No one knows that, except you."

Ben shook his head, ever so slightly, a glint of something warm, and tender, yet serious, behind his bottomless dark eyes. *Like-like-like-like* pulsed through Nora's head like an anthem.

"I know you are no pushover, Nora, but that doesn't mean you have to act as if you're indestructible. That if you own up to even a modicum of fragility, you'll be hit from all sides by a fleet of Mack trucks."

If only he knew he was the Mack truck. That

she was struck, and continued to be struck, every day she knew him.

"Can't a girl simply like muffins?" she asked, grateful to find words that didn't make her look like the puddle she'd become.

As if he knew she needed a little extra fortification, he laid his hands on her, resting, warm and secure on her upper arms. Then he pulled her in, his arms sliding around her shoulders. Hers—oh, so naturally—slid around his back.

"I didn't mean to upset you, Nora. I just want you to know that you deserve more than people in your past might have led you to believe you deserve."

"I know."

"Promise me you'll learn to say no."

"No."

His laughter rolled through her like a summer storm, fast and invigorating.

Nora tilted her head so the side of her face pressed up against Ben's chest. She'd have pressed deeper, pressed till all of herself was up against all of him if it were physically possible.

Because while it was something she'd spent her entire adult life telling herself she'd never crave, never need, never find, she knew what *like-like-like-like* meant. And now she'd felt it, now it was a part of her, she knew she had to hold on to it as tightly as she could, soaking up every skerrick, until it was taken away.

When Ben lifted his arm, she might have whimpered just a little. When he used a finger to tilt her face, when he smiled down at her before laying his mouth over hers, the whimper turned into a sigh.

Later, as she lay back in Ben's arms in her big, soft bed, her leg curled over his, her fingers making tracks through the hair on his chest as he checked his phone for work emails, her mind tracked back over the conversations of the day.

Little Red Riding Hood amongst other things. Ben lounging in the doorway. Ben tensing any time talk strayed to his relationship with Clancy. Ben intimating that he thought Clancy might have taken advantage of her good nature.

He cared. He felt protective towards her. That much was clear.

But some bigger part of the conversation felt undone. As if she'd missed an opportunity to get to the bottom of it all. For while Ben had seen to the very heart of her, over and over again, been witness to every one of her insecurities, she still had no clue why Ben and Clancy had fallen out.

It had to be intentional. Was he just that hard to crack? Or was it that she wasn't the kind of person people ever let close? Not when she was pushy and brazen, or since she'd learnt how to be sunshiny and soft.

While she'd spent years telling herself it didn't

matter, that it was okay, that she could cope, it turned out she was lying to herself the whole time.

It hurt. It hurt so bad.

Nora yawned, scrubbing some life into her scalp as she flicked through her morning emails. When she opened the third, her jaw all but dislocated when it fell open in shock.

It was a job offer, by way of a competition she'd entered. Six months working at a resort in Far North Queensland on a social-media take-over. She'd be paid, and pretty well too, for experiencing every adventure the region had to offer, and posting about it.

It was the opportunity of a lifetime for a fledgling social-media sort like her. And it started two weeks from now.

Nora glanced quickly towards the en suite when she heard the shower turn on. And had the strange sense that it was something she ought to discuss with Ben.

But no. No discussions. This was her thing. Alone. And the timing could not have been more perfect.

Because she had fallen in love with Ben Hawthorne.

He, on the other hand, clearly had no clue, trundling around the house with the exact same comportment as the day they'd met: with grace, and strength, and a locked box where his heart should be.

She must have made a noise, or was sending anxious waves into the universe, as Cutie lifted his head from his position on the end of her bed. Pie, snuggled up beside him, slept through, not giving a jot as to Nora's cares.

"It's okay," she said, and Cutie cocked his head. "In fact, it's brilliant. The universe has pointed the way to my next adventure. Great news, huh?"

Cutie shook his head and snuffled—a goodly amount of saliva flying across the room and landing on the wall, the floor, a lamp—then he lay back down and closed his eyes.

She shook her head too, managing to keep all saliva locked away, then read over the email one more time.

The packing list was laptop, beachwear, and a six-month supply of sunscreen. Even less than her usual minimalist fare. And she already owned a kaftan! Slow lifestyle, sunshine, impermanent population; it was the polar opposite of the bustling community that she'd spent her last year and a half falling in love with. The perfect cathartic cleansing.

A sound came from the bathroom. It was Ben. Humming. No, *singing*, in the shower—"Blue Moon", no less—that hot, deep, sexy voice of his terribly out of tune. And she had to admit, he wasn't *exactly* the same man he'd been when he'd shown up at Clancy's front door. He walked the place in bare feet, eating peanut butter from the jar, lying back on the too small couch with his feet over the arm rest. All things happy people did. People who felt content. Comfortable.

But still, not lovesick.

Meaning her job here was done.

She pressed *reply* and began to type an effusive yes, but then stopped herself. There was no need to be rash. First she'd read the fine print. Figure out her finances. Check if there was a non-compete clause. Would she be able to keep *The Girl Upstairs* going at the same time? The exposure would be fabulous, but she didn't want to leave her current clients in the lurch.

With that, slowly, achingly slowly, she closed her laptop. Stood. Wiped dry palms down the sides of her shorts.

When Ben's phone lit up the caller was listed as *World's Best Assistant*. Damon. *Ha.*

When Ben started up "Smoke Gets in Your Eyes", after a half-second hesitation, she answered.

"Hey, Damon."

A beat, then, "Nora? That you?"

"'Tis me."

"Well, what do you know? The boss man around?"

The humming from the shower continued. "He's indisposed. Can I pass on a message?"

"I guess. But first where is he, and why are you answering his phone?"

"None of your business, boyo."

"I know you say that, but I feel as if I was a big part of getting the two of you together—"

"We're not together." They weren't. They really weren't. But the thought of *actually* leaving him made Nora's heart clutch.

"Right," said Damon, the tone of his voice making it clear he didn't actually believe her either. "My message is twofold. First, he wanted the name of some local real estate agents. Do you have a pencil?"

"Ah…"

"Long sticky-looking thing you can write things down with?"

"Got it." Nora grabbed a pencil, while her mind quietly spun about in even more frantic circles.

"Okay, this company had the best rep when it came to honest valuations," said Damon, naming a local group.

Valuations? Valuation meant *selling*. Was Ben selling Thornfield Hall and hadn't mentioned it to her? *Just like you planned to move to Far North Queensland without discussing it with him?*

"Not the same thing."

"What's that, now?" Damon asked.

"Nothing. I've got it."

Yeah, she got it all right. Ben was selling Thornfield Hall and he hadn't deemed it something she might like to know. Just as he'd made a concerted effort not to tell her why he was still so upset with Clancy. Damon knew the former. Everyone else around her seemed to know the latter. Leaving her on the outside, looking in. Again.

"What was the other thing?"

Damon paused. "You know what, I'll save that one for when he calls back."

Nora's phone rang. She glanced at it as she said, "Are you sure?"

"I'm sure," said Damon. "Thanks. Make good choices!"

"You bet," she sing-songed before hanging up, out of habit rather than any real sense of sunshine, as her well seemed to have completely dried up.

Her phone rang again. She answered, "The Girl Upstairs."

"Hey, Nora? It's Gemma from Playful Paws. Good news! We've found a home for Cutie and Pie! A young couple on the Peninsula. Big yard. Near the beach. She has a small business making baby food, works from home."

Nora slowly sat on the bed.

"Oh!" said Nora, her gaze flicking to the patchy, scratchy, bitsy dogs curled up on the end of her bed.

Gemma went on, "The photo you put on your Insta went crazy. We had so many expressions of interest we were able to pick and choose where they are going. Though, it has to be said, several of the phone calls were expressions of interest in the guy."

The guy being Ben. Eyes crinkled, huge smile on his face, as he crouched down to make eye contact with Pie. Cutie in the background, head cocked. *The Girl Upstairs* knew how to sell "likeable" like no one else.

She ran a hand over her eyes, as they suddenly felt gritty and so very tired. "I'm so happy. They sound…perfect."

Suddenly the singing stopped. Then the shower. Then Nora's heart seemed to give up right along with it.

She smacked herself in the chest. Then said, "Sorry, I have to zoom. Message me the details and I'll make sure they're ready to go when you're ready to take them."

"Will do. Thanks again, Nora. You're the best. We literally could not have done this without you."

Nora hung up without saying goodbye, her throat too tight to form anything other than some kind of strangled grunt.

To think that where she used to hear, "You're a lot, Nora. Too loud. Too much," now she heard, "You're the best. We literally could not have done this without you." So why did it feel like the same thing?

"Nora?"

Nora jumped out of her skin.

"You still here?"

She bit her lip to keep the ever so slightly hysterical laugh to herself, then managed, "Yep. I'm still here."

"Good. Now take your clothes off, because I have plans!"

The door swung open and with it came a waft of steam, and Ben; towel slung low around his waist, a pair of water droplets sliding down his buff chest, water making his eyelashes tangle and curl.

Her heart squeezed at the sight of him. At the love that swirled about her insides like brandy on a cold night. She'd never imagined love could ache like this. But when it was only one way, it hurt like crazy.

If only she'd never made that promise to Clancy that she'd look after the house till the new owner took it off her hands. She would have never heard of Ben Hawthorne. Never have reached out. Never have emailed, or rung, or video-chatted. Never have cajoled him into coming back. Never have met him, kissed him, snuggled up to him on the couch, made love to him. Seen him in that towel.

Never have spent the last few weeks with a pair of butty dogs, and a house to call home and…and the man she loved sleeping in her bed.

She'd never have lived the dream she'd never dared have.

Or lost it all in one fell swoop.

"Why are you still dressed?" he asked.

And when he lifted an eyebrow, his mouth quirking adorably, Nora burst into tears.

CHAPTER TWELVE

NORA THOUGHT IT safest to let Ben think her melt-down was about the dogs.

At which point he took over. Completely. Which, actually, was a blessed relief as the afternoon had completely sapped her. She could barely remember what sunshine even felt like, much less conjured up enough to put on a brave face.

Ben gave them both a last bath—Cutie in the yard, Pie in the laundry sink, his eyes glinting lovingly at Ben the entire time. He gathered their toys, washed their bedding, didn't get upset when the newly fixed washing machine broke once again. Not once did he look at her sideways, or make a big deal of the fact that she sat on the floor watching and crying. Crying as if she might never stop.

Then it was over. Gemma came around in a cute little pink van with the Playful Paws logo on the side. And—with Ben and Nora's help—loaded

Cutie, Pie and all the paraphernalia they had collected over the past few weeks into the back.

"I travel lighter than they do," Nora managed.

Ben stepped up beside her, put a strong, warm arm around hers shoulders, and kissed her atop her head. "You're not giving them up," he said as Gemma beeped the horn and raced away. "You were a warm, kind, protective space, readying them for their for-ever family. They'd never have found one another, if not for your patience and your kindness."

Her love for the guy doubled, just like that.

When, later that night, Ben fell asleep in front of *The Sting*, her hands playing with his hair, her gaze tracing the contours of his beautiful nose, his tangled lashes, his strong jaw, she told herself the only reason she hadn't yet told him about her job offer, or Damon's phone call, wasn't because she was keeping things from him,

But because she'd only burst into tears again, and this time not have a safe excuse.

"Nora!" Ben called, his deep voice curling its way up the stairs.

"Ben," she muttered back, lifting her head a smidge from where it had been resting on her forearms on her desk. She felt as if she was coming down with something. Was there a tablet to cure the doldrums?

She heard Ben's feet taking the stairs two at a

time. She winced as she waited for him to trip—
but no, the man was too lithe for that to happen
unless she was the one tumbling into him. Taking him down.

"Why didn't you tell me Damon rang yesterday?" he asked as he burst into the room.

Nora nibbled at her bottom lip. "I forgot?"
Yeah, okay, so the lilt at the end of her sentence
made it clear that wasn't entirely the case.

She prepared to bat her lashes his way—she
couldn't quite muster the energy to do much
else—but in the end she gave up and put her
head back on the desk.

"Hey," he said, his voice dropping. She felt
the air shift as he moved her way. "What's going
on? Is it the dogs? Gemma said we could visit
any time." He put a hand on her forehead. "You
haven't been yourself the last couple of days."

Not wanting to be a bother, she pressed herself to sitting and turned on the chair, leaning her
arms across the back. "I'm fine. While you've
been a busy boy."

"It's the house," said Ben, moving to sit on the
end of the bed.

"I can't believe you're selling it, after all the
progress you've made here."

"I'm considering my options. And what do you
mean by progress?"

"With *Clancy*," she said, throwing her arms
out to the side. "You seem to have made so much

headway, telling stories about her without my having to nudge, no longer frowning when her name is mentioned."

"Nora, sweetheart, come on," he said, reaching for her.

"Don't sweetheart me!"

Ben pulled his hand away, his expression wary, as if she were about to go rabid. Which she just might.

She knew that tone all too well. It was the I'm-about-to-disappoint-you tone.

"You're upset," he said.

"You think? I'm furious." And she was. Suddenly she was pacing, back and forth, at the end of her bed. "I'm furious with myself. I've been such a fool."

"Regarding?"

"You!"

She waved both hands in his direction, and his hand lifted to rub against this mouth, as if he could sense what was truly front and centre on her mind. As if she could tell him the truths he'd assured her he'd always want to hear.

But she baulked. Deflected. "You didn't want to talk about Clancy, so I left it alone. Let you set the pace. That's not what I do. Why? Because it always bites me on the ass. All this time, all this work, and you're just going to sell the house."

"I'm just considering it. You want me to tell

you about Clancy?" he said, his voice rough, a muscle ticcing in his cheek.

"Are you kidding me?"

Ben shook his head. "If it's that important to you, I'll tell you anything you want to know."

"Anything?"

He nodded.

And for a second, a brief suspended moment in time, with his dark, serious, warm, kind eyes locked onto hers, she once again felt as if she *could* ask him anything. Did he have feelings for her? What scared him most in the world? Would they ever see one another again?

But her self-protective instincts had been slumbering of late, basking in the warm glow of having Ben near, and now, as familiar feelings of being pushed into a corner ramped up inside her, it was almost a relief to feel those instincts come back to life.

"Tell me about Clancy," she demanded. "Tell me what happened between you. Because it is eating me up inside to think the two of you, two people whom I...respect and admire, were so at odds that it ended the way it did, and I can't take it any more."

There, that felt better. No more pussyfooting around. It was time they had this out. Because time was running out.

Nora had no clue she was crying again until a tear fell past the edge of her lip, the salty taste touching her tongue. She swiped it away, her gaze fierce, hoping he couldn't see in her eyes the ache that whatever it was they'd shared these past weeks was coming to an end.

Ben dropped his face into both hands and sat there, his gaze faraway, his skin stretched tight over his bones. He looked ravaged, and it had happened so fast.

It was nearly enough for Nora to drop to her knees, to take his hands in hers and tell him to forget it. To spend what time they had left snuggling and eating homemade tacos and making love.

But then he said, "I wasn't adopted."

"I'm sorry?"

"Clancy did not adopt me. She was my actual grandmother. My mother's mother."

Knees losing functionality, Nora sat gingerly on the corner of the bed. "I don't understand. She said—"

"I know what she said. I know what everyone said. How selfless she was for taking in a quiet, serious five-year-old kid. At her age."

"But she was your mother's *mother*? For real?"

Ben breathed out hard once more. "She was. You asked me once if Clancy had a Rochester of her own. She did. My grandfather."

"Gerald," Nora whispered, the name coming back to her from overheard stage whispers between the widows.

"He was a war correspondent. Clever guy, quite well known in his time. Died, overseas, when Clancy was pregnant with my mother. They hadn't married, but turned out he'd changed his will, leaving her this house. His family tried to fight it, but Clancy stood strong. She had a child to raise, after all. Aida Hawthorne. My mother."

Nora's head spun. What a thing to discover. "But surely that's a happy lie?"

Ben's gaze seemed locked in the past, as if he wasn't seeing the room in front of him at all. "When my mother left me on Clancy's doorstep, she told me she was going away for a while, but she'd be back. The one time I asked Clancy when that might be, she told me my parents were both dead. The truth was she'd told my mother that if she walked away, she was never to darken the door again. I figured that's why the adoption ruse—Clancy was ashamed at what my mother had given up. The only reason I even know that much is because I happened upon Clancy when she was told the news that Aida had died."

And Ben. Oh, Ben. *That* was why the armour. The desire for truth. The slow, measured, deliberate decisions. Poor guy was always waiting for the axe to fall.

Clancy, what were you thinking?

"How are you so functional?" she mumbled. "How are you so together?"

His dark gaze swung to her and her heart went

off; beating like crazy for this big, clever, generous man with his big, beautiful broken heart.

"I was," he finally said, his gaze travelling over her face as if committing it to memory. "I was functional, I was *fine*, till you dragged me out here to rehash all this stuff."

His cheek twitched; a smile, even now. Another sign of his immense fortitude. His wonderfulness. His determination to protect her from his baser feelings.

But she didn't need protection. Not from that. Not from him.

"I'm so sorry," she said, her voice gravelly. "I'm sorry for forcing you to come here."

"I'm not."

Heat flashed in his eyes, leant weight to his words. And had her fingers curling into the blanket.

"Besides," he said, "I'm the one who needs to apologise to you. For not being there to look after my imprudent grandmother when she was sick. That should never have fallen to you."

"It wasn't your fault. No one knew."

Ben shook his head. "That's the thing. Clancy did. She knew she was sick, long before she let on."

Nora's mouth dropped open, but she didn't know where to start. Ben's words made no sense.

Ben clasped his hand behind his neck, the

muscles tight. "I suspect Clancy knew she had cancer for some time."

Nora shook her head. "No. That's not right. She might have felt *unwell* on occasion, tired easily, but she didn't get an actual diagnosis until a few weeks before she died."

"She knew. She knew before you moved in."

"Before...?" Like a combination lock clicking into place Nora realised what Ben was suggesting. "No. I don't believe you."

"Those recipe books we found at the back of the pantry. They were hers. She was a great cook. Her dinner parties were what originally brought people to the house."

"Are you saying she took me in, as a tenant, knowing she was unwell? That I paid rent for the privilege of taking care of her?"

Ben nodded.

Nora's hand shook as it covered her mouth. The first person, the *one* person, she'd ever let herself believe loved her for her, and it was all a ruse. "She saw me coming from a mile away."

A tear slipped down her cheek, then another.

"Nora, honey, don't cry. Dammit. I never wanted to ruin your good opinion of Clancy, which was the only reason I kept it from you. But you just seemed so determined to know. And I didn't want to hide anything from you, not any more, as I know how that feels. And..."

Ben swore beneath his breath, his expression even more ravaged than it had been before. "Look, if it's any consolation, if she saw you coming from a mile away it wouldn't have been due to any desire to dupe you. She'd have never wanted a nurse. Or sympathy. She'd have taken one look at you, felt your youth, your vitality, your assertiveness, and figured that's how she wanted to spend her last days: alongside a fearless young woman who carries muffins through deep dark woods, despite any and all danger to herself."

Ben shifted closer, waited till her eyes snagged on his.

"For all that I wish she were here now, so I could have a piece of her for what she did to you, I understand that want. The urge to soak in all that you have to offer, all that you are, even temporarily. You are a force, Nora Letterman, whether it feels like it right now or not."

Nora knew he was trying to make it better, but all she could do was shake her head. It was too much. The dogs, the house, the rewriting of the past. Her feelings for Ben all tangled and hard.

Ben reached out to brush a strand of hair behind her ear, as if she was right there beside him, when really she was outside her own body, leaving room for him to add, "I might have been able to forgive her for not telling me about my mother, but I'll never forgive her for what she did to you. Never."

Nora came back into her own body with a whoosh.

She was mortified. And pissed. And embarrassed as hell. But she'd been on the receiving end of so much bad news over the years, she knew that, while it felt immediate, and sharp, right now, she'd live.

But Ben. Ben looked changed. As if telling her had taken something from him. As if he was honestly more upset about Clancy duping her than lying to him.

Meaning everything she'd done to help Ben reconcile with Clancy—staying, reaching out, opening up, giving up so much of herself to the cause that she'd fallen in love with the man—it would all be for nothing.

He *had* to forgive Clancy. And the only way that was possible was if he let it all go. The house. His anger. And her.

While her tears dried on her face, a sense of clarity came over her. Not the clarity of sunshine, but the clarity of survival.

This was no different from any other time she'd hit a crossroads; it was time for her to jump before she was pushed.

Before she could change her mind, she wiped away one last tear, steeled herself, and blurted, "In some better news, I got a job."

"A job," he parroted.

"Well, an amazing opportunity, really," she

said, doing a mighty fine job of not sounding as if she was paddling like mad beneath the water. "A social-media takeover at a resort in Far North Queensland. It starts in a little under two weeks, but I can head up there as soon as I please. Yay."

Ben reared back as if she'd taken a swipe at him. "When did this happen?"

"I applied a while ago. I got the news yesterday."

His eyes roved over her face as if looking for something. A way in. Or a way out. Then something seemed to shift. To dislodge. Leaving him open. And with a flash that felt like a knife between the ribs she saw his hurt. Deep, cavernous, ancient and immediate. If they looked anything like this when Clancy had ripped off the Band-Aid regarding her truth, she'd never have forgiven herself.

"So, you're taking it?" he said. "Just like that. Please tell me this isn't some knee-jerk reaction to what I just told you."

"It's not. It's real. And I can hardly say no."

Something in her words snagged him. She saw it in his eyes. A flicker. A sense of hope. "But is it what you want?"

"Sure. I mean, it sounds fine. Great, actually. A once-in-a-lifetime chance."

What did it *matter*? He'd come to Fitzroy for her. She'd stayed in Fitzroy for him. And it had been magical. But now she had to go. And he had to let her. So he'd forgive Clancy. And so she could move on, knowing she'd done all she could to leave the situation better than when she'd found it.

"Come on, Ben, we're almost done here. And you're leaving anyway." Ugh. She'd almost made it through before her voice broke on the last word.

"Are you saying...you want me to stay?"

Did she? Yes. *Yes, yes, yes.* Could she? Not in a million years. Even while the thought of walking away from him made her feel as if she were tearing out a rib, she bit her tongue and said nothing.

People weren't to be trusted with their own feelings. Look at Nora: when the going got tough, she left. How could she ever expect Ben not to do the same?

"Look, we'll talk later. I have to meet Misty. Promised her I'd do a thing. So, I'll see you in a bit, okay?"

Eyes welling, she quickly turned, went downstairs, headed out of the broken back door to find it was no longer broken. There was a new lock. With a key on the inside. She used it to scurry through the back garden and out into the alley behind the terrace houses.

And she walked. She walked and walked, away from their little street. Past houses she'd never seen, parks she'd never traversed.

It was all so unfamiliar it felt as if she'd already moved on.

* * *

When Nora came home later, the house was quiet bar the murmur of Ben's voice from his room as he spoke to someone, probably Damon, probably about work stuff. The important stuff in his actual life, back in London.

When he didn't come to her bed that night, she lay awake, imagining his long frame curled up on the small single bed downstairs. Wondering if he was lying there in the dark, thinking about her too, till it became too much so she got up and started to pack.

And while she wished she could turn back time, and redo that entire hot mess of a conversation, she consoled herself with the fact that, right now, she was exactly where she'd hoped to be at the very beginning.

Ben had faced his issues with Clancy. And she finally had a way out.

Yippee.

Nora's two small bags were sitting at the front door early the next morning.

In a brief flare of insight, she wondered when having so little had become a kind of flag to wave when really it only served to make her appear smaller and less of an imposition. As if that were the best gift she could give those she left behind.

In the end it was a lie. Because the memories she'd collected in this place filled ten times that much space. Her heart clutched so hard at the thought of walking away from them all, she rubbed the heel of her palm into her chest.

Speaking of people, Nora turned to find Ben leaning against the kitchen doorjamb in a Henley T and soft jeans. Barefoot with a little stubble on his usually clean-cut cheeks, a tuft of hair sitting not quite right, as if he'd tossed and turned as much as she had.

"Running away from home?" he asked.

God, he was beautiful. And kind. And forgiving. While she couldn't be sure how long it would take her to get over him, to get over this whole place, and everything that had happened here, he'd be so fine.

She mustered a wobbly smile. "Despite appearances, I wasn't going to leave without saying goodbye. I'm staying at Misty's for a couple of days. Something I probably should have done earlier. To give you the space you needed to focus on what was important."

Something hot and dark flashed behind his eyes. "And what is that, exactly?"

"Reconciling yourself with your grandmother, of course. Last night you seemed to make some giant leaps in that direction. Leaps you might have made sooner without me pressing and prodding in all the wrong places, or making you lose focus on what mattered to you. I fear my being here made things...muddy."

"Muddy, you say."

"I do. I do say that. I can be a lot. Sunshine or no sunshine, I can be a lot. And while I'm slowly becoming more and more okay with that, you need to just be alone here. To say goodbye."

His chest lifted and fell. Then his strong arms folded over his chest. "I've never much liked goodbyes," he said.

"Me neither. But they are a fact of life." She shrugged. What more was there to say? "Anything you need me to do, before I go, just let me know."

"Don't go," Ben said, his eyes serious. His words harking back to another time he'd said nearly the same thing. "Not yet."

With a soft shrug she gave him one last part of herself. "For years, I'd wake up every morning, waiting for someone to tap me on the shoulder and tell me I didn't belong there. The thing is, I *knew* I didn't belong there. I don't belong anywhere, and I've always been okay with that. But here? With you? I forgot. I forgot myself. I forgot my limits.

"I've been living someone else's life and it's time I start living mine again."

She grabbed her backpack and slung it over

her shoulder. Then took her battered old suitcase and held tight to the handle.

For a breath she thought they might move as one towards the middle; she could all but feel him in her arms. But neither moved.

She gave him a smile and reached for the door handle. Then turned at the last.

"Clancy called your name, the second last day, maybe the third. Did I ever tell you that?"

Ben shook his head, slowly.

"I think she thought I was you. Looking after her. At the end."

Ben's chin dropped, the muscles in his neck tensing, and he said, "She didn't need me. She had you."

"She needed you, Ben. She loved you. She missed you. She just didn't know how to tell you."

Nora wondered if Clancy had seen that in her too. If part of her appeal was that they were both useless when it came to expressing how they truly felt. If she'd felt she needed someone, at the end, who wouldn't judge. Would simply hold her hand.

"Thank you," Nora said. "For telling me about Clancy. For trusting me with your story. For not protecting me from mine."

She locked eyes with his, saw way too much understanding therein. He knew how she felt. Knew why she had to leave. He had to.

For the first time ever, she'd met someone who was too much for her.

With a watery smile, she grabbed the door handle, walked out onto the patio and was gone.

CHAPTER THIRTEEN

BEN STOOD ON the threshold of the sitting room at Thornfield Hall, eyes glancing off the fireplace, the ottoman, the bookshelves that had been well cleaned out by the Widows' Book Club, and found himself in an unfamiliar position.

He had not a single clue what he should do next.

For as long as he could remember, from when he woke up in the morning to the moment he finally fell asleep, he felt sure of his actions. As if he had some kind of moral divining rod in his subconscious that let him know he was on the right path. If, at one point, that metaphorical rod had spoken with Clancy's voice, well, then, it was what it was.

But now? Nothing. Take a step forward? Step back? Scratch his nose? Clear his throat? Give up or go hard, book a flight back to London tonight and put the damn house on the market or stay a few more days and finish what he'd begun?

It was as if the divining rod had turned its

metaphorical back on him right as he felt as if he were in the centre of some centrifugal vortex. Now whatever he decided to do would spin him off in a direction from which he'd never return.

The *spinning* had begun the moment Nora had left, with her backpack and battered little suitcase. Her tilted chin and brave smile no match for the heartache and disenchantment written all over her face.

For a moment, he'd believed that heartache had been all his. That her feelings for him might even come close to matching his own for her. But she'd never been one to hold back, so he'd had to assume he was projecting.

So, London. Surely his next move was London. They were just fine, for now. The Zoom meeting he'd set up moments after Nora's departure, so that he had something to do other than stare at the door and will it to sweep open with her on the other side, had seen Damon and the team tumbling over one another like puppies to get out the good news about how much work they'd been able to achieve.

But they'd need him soon. Him and his cape.

Twelve-hour days, meetings and working lunches, falling asleep on the couch with his coat on, alone, seemed like a different world. A different life. And yet getting back to work would be a welcome distraction from the constant low-

level ache that had descended over his body after
Nora had walked out of the door. Surely.

For she'd left. She'd really left. After all she'd
done to get him here, she'd actually walked away.

Sure, she'd *told* him she would, from the very
first time they'd spoken. It hadn't come out of
thin air. And yet he hadn't seen it coming.

He'd been far too busy loving her. Distracted
entirely by the falling, the surprise of it, the rich-
ness, the joy. Assuming all the while that she'd
been feeling the same. Maybe not quite so fast,
maybe not with quite such easy acceptance, but
they'd been falling together. And while he hadn't
had a plan, he'd been okay with that. Not having
a plan when he'd hopped on the plane to Melbourne had led to the time of his life.

Only now she was gone.

And he didn't know what to do about it.

His first experience with feeling loved had
gone to Clancy. Her version all about control.
Hanging on tight. Too tight. He understood now
that its origins hadn't given her much room to
move, and in the end it had suffocated him.

What choice had he had other than to love
Nora a whole other way? By giving her space,
and time, and room. By being truthful, brutally
so if necessary, but not pressing, not over-shar-
ing. If she wanted to go, then surely, even if it
cut him to pieces, loving her meant letting her
make that choice.

But, damn, it hurt.

Needing to feel something other than heartache, Ben took a step inside the very room in which he and Clancy had had their God-awful falling out. He could picture himself standing there, he could see her wonderful familiar face, wretched with apology, yet determined that if she'd had to make the same choice, she'd make it again. Because look at him. Look at the man he'd become.

But it was also the room in which he and Nora had watched a dozen movies he could barely remember, as he'd been far too focussed on her fingers making gentle tracks through his hair. The way her eyes crinkled and her mouth hooked when something whimsical happened on screen. The way she'd burst into laughter any time the dogs let off wind in their sleep and raced him out of the room.

Whatever secrets it had kept hidden, this house had always been a safe place for those who felt at sea. But despite Nora's hopes, it wasn't his home. Not any more. The only person who'd made him feel at home in a very long time had walked out of his door. And he'd let her.

She'd made her move. In pure survival mode, she'd left before she could be told it was time to go.

The ball was in his court.

And with that Ben felt a small shift in perception, like a glimpse of sunlight through a rain cloud. Maybe there was a happy medium. He'd read enough of Clancy's book-club reads as a teen to know that love was meant to uplift and illuminate. Maybe there was some way he could hold Nora tight, and also give her space to be whoever she wanted to be.

The ball was in his court.

But he'd asked her to stay. No, he'd said, "Don't go. Not yet"—a very different thing to a woman who'd been asked to leave more foster homes than she could count—when what he should have said was, "If you want this, if you want me, if you choose to come to me, as I chose to find you, if you're willing to take the risk on trusting me, I will love you and never leave you," over and over until she had not a single doubt.

The ball was in his court.

The divining rod inside him was back, with a vengeance.

"Did you hear?"

"Now what?" Nora snapped, not looking up from her laptop as she flicked between reading the contract the resort island had sent for the hundredth time and checking out the many ways she could get out of town fast.

Not that they'd changed in the couple of days she'd been holed up at Misty's, waiting in case she got a phone call from a certain person asking for her help.

"Feisty," said Misty. "Yet you were such a droopy Dora when you turned up on my doorstep, all maudlin after your day of self-sabotage."

Nora rolled her eyes, and twisted her back, sore from having spent a few nights on Misty's couch in the tiny apartment above her shop. "It wasn't self-sabotage. It's called 'putting a family back together'," Nora said, wishing she hadn't told Misty a thing.

But the moment she'd walked into Vintage Vamp, the first tear had dropped, then the next, then suddenly it was all over red rover. Misty had closed the shop and taken Nora up the side stairs, shoved her on the couch, brought her a tub of Jamoca Almond Fudge ice cream and let her cry and vent enough over the past twenty-four hours to drown herself.

At least the lack of sleep had given her plenty of time to mull.

Over Clancy.

Even knowing there was a fair chance Clancy had taken advantage of her good nature, if Nora knew anything to be true, it was that surviving was hard, and people had to do it the best way they knew how. She'd loved living in that house, and if she had to do it all again, she'd not have changed a thing.

She'd mulled over her future. Six months of

cocktails and free steak dinners and sand in the crotch of her bikini. It'd be great. Lonely, though, and far away from a whole bunch of people she'd come to like. *Like*-like, in fact.

And she'd mulled over Ben. She'd done that most of all.

Turned out love was not a tap you could simply shut off just because you'd decided it was too hot. Every time she thought of him, it hurt. Every time Misty turned on the radio and Nora thought she heard his voice, it hurt. Every time she imagined how things might have gone down differently if she weren't such a messed-up scaredy-cat, it hurt.

But what else could she have done with a man so stubborn and dry? Who worked far too hard. Who snored, just a little, and couldn't sit through a single romantic comedy.

A man who liked to sleep closest to the door, and who didn't tell her when he was putting in a new lock because he knew she'd protest. Who didn't even blink when a one-eared, one-eyed, raggedy mutt rubbed noses with him.

A man who'd travelled halfway around the world to face his biggest heartache, because he wanted to be there when she faced hers.

Yes, her feelings for the guy had been overwhelming. Because *he* was overwhelming. Her subconscious had been right to see danger where he was concerned. And if she'd thrown every missile she had in his direction, and in the end only shot herself in the foot, okay, yes, one might call that self-sabotage.

But she was who she was. And if he couldn't handle that, then so be it.

The beaches of Far North Queensland it was.

And, boy, didn't she sound excited about the prospect, even to her own ear?

Knowing she'd not absorb a single word once her mind went down this path, Nora breathed out hard and slowly lowered the lid of her laptop. She stood and dragged her hands through her hair. Then, in need of a distraction, she met Misty in her kitchen as she reached up to bang the smoke detector when the toaster set it off.

"What were you saying before?" Nora asked. "Did you hear…?"

"Right. Did you hear, Ben—?"

Nora held up a hand. "Nope. Sorry. But nope. I've dealt with enough rumours and secrets about that man to last a lifetime."

Misty's mouth worked silently, her body rocking side to side as if she was struggling to contain her news, till Nora was hit with the awful feeling she already knew.

"It's about the house, right?"

Misty nodded.

"It's on the market." Ben had probably put the terrace house up for sale the moment she'd walked out of the door. And gone back to London. Without looking back. It was the soundtrack of her life, after all.

"Wrong."

"Wrong?"

"He's given it to us!"

"I'm sorry, what?"

"Ben! Your big, beautiful, mountainous hottie. At first he seemed too serious for me, but now I do believe he's a saint."

"What are you talking about?"

"He's not selling, you numpty, he's giving Clancy's place over to the community. As a community space. He wants us to be able to continue to use it as a place for people to gather, to come together, for free. Book clubs. The Garden Club. Play groups. Puppy play groups. He said you gave him the idea. He's going to fund a mini renovation, make sure it's sturdy and functional, while keeping its cool Clancy vibe. And he's asked if I'll administrate."

Oh. Oh, Ben. That was…beyond. Perfect. Generous. Clancy would have been so proud.

"Hey… Hey… *Hey!*" said Misty, moving in and hovering over Nora, before hugging her awkwardly around her head. "No more tears. Please. I can't stand it."

"I'm not—" Nora swiped her cheek to find it dry. She was done with tears. Truly.

Misty lifted away, a hand moving to Nora's face, before she said, "He said not to tell you."

Nora flinched. "Ben said that? Why?"

"He said if you knew you'd decide to stay, at least for a while. To help get things in order. Because you know you'd be awesome at it. Which he knew too, but that wasn't the point. The point was, you needed to be where *you* wanted to be. No strings. No caveats. No taking care of others. No hanging around to help him, or be with him, or so that he could be with you. If any of us told you, we'd have him to deal with. But since when have I ever done what some man told me to do?"

"Never," Nora whispered, her head spinning.

What was Ben playing at? He *knew* Misty would tell her. That she'd delight in passing on every word.

It was a sign. He'd given her a *sign*.

She looked to her tattoo. *Footloose and fancy-free.* A dandelion on the wind. That was the only signpost she'd followed for years. And right now it could take her to some gorgeous island resort for six months where she'd feel lonely and miserable.

Imagining herself out in the world with Ben, on the other hand—pretending to understand modern art, playing footsies under the table in some café, or snuggled on a couch, slowly turning one another on—made her feel alive, and tangible and just a little scared.

But it was a good scared. The kind born of anticipation.

She was in love with the man. From the desk of, in the bed of, nose to nose, in heated disagreement with, and everything in between. They'd delighted in nights of quiet and weathered emotional storms. She'd cooked while he'd washed up. They'd never once fought over the remote. And even as she'd walked out on him, it had been done with kindness, and generosity and love. On both sides.

Ben had given her a sign. He wanted her to come home.

Only home wasn't any place she'd ever belonged. It was Ben. All Ben.

She moved so fast she banged into Misty's kitchen table, and somehow caught her laptop before it fell to the floor. "I'll be back for this. Some time."

"No more tears?" Misty asked, her gaze far too clever for her own good.

"No more tears," said Nora.

"Atta girl."

CHAPTER FOURTEEN

NORA STOOD OUTSIDE Thornfield Hall, thinking back to the last time she'd really stopped to take it in. The beautiful fretwork, the creeping jasmine. A little love and understanding, and a lick of new paint, and it would truly shine.

"Okay," Nora said, shaking out her hands and rolling her neck. "No more waiting. You're done waiting. You've waited your whole life to meet someone who liked you, and accepted you, just the way you were. So go get him."

A new mantra beating in her head, she walked up the path.

At the front door, she pulled her phone out of her tote. Brought up Ben's number. Took a moment to gaze at his contact profile, a sneaky pic she'd taken of him while he was sleeping: his face half hidden by the pillow, the half you could see enough to make a girl's heart tumble.

Taking a deep breath, she pressed the call button, then shook her hair off her shoulder, put the phone to her ear, and hoped against hope that this time, of all the times, she'd read the signs right.

It was worth the risk.

The ringtone ceased, then came a pause that seemed to last for ever before a familiar deep voice said, "Where are you?"

Nora felt a ball of sunshine spontaneously appear in her belly. With those three little words she spun back in time to their first phone calls and video chats, when she'd actually believed she'd only been checking in with him daily because it was her duty. When all the while she'd actually been adoring him, wooing him, in her own clumsy way. And he'd never once called her on it. Not once. When it must have been obvious as hell.

"I'm out front," she said, her voice breathless. Despite all efforts to stay cool, there was no stopping the feelings this man brought out in her. The warm delight. The hope. No fairy dust required. "I'm… I'm home."

No response. She looked to the phone to find he'd hung up. She heard footsteps, as if they were coming down the stairs, then the door flew open.

And there he was.

It had been a few days since she'd seen those warm eyes, that face—so handsome it took every effort not to squint in the presence of so much gorgeousness—but it felt like for ever.

"Hi," he said.

"Hi." She wondered if she looked as hungry as

he did as he drank her in, eyes tracking her old yellow T with its pink tractor motif, the small hole in the hem covered by the knot at her belly, the long floral skirt Misty had thrown at her when she'd nearly run out of the door in just her T-shirt and undies.

"How've you been?" he asked when his gaze once more connected with hers.

"Crap. You?"

The edge of Ben's mouth twitched, then curled, and then he laughed, the sound so rich and warm and delicious it was all she could do not to throw herself at him, bury her face in his neck and move in.

"Were you upstairs, just now?" she asked, peering about the corner.

He let out a long slow breath, before admitting, "I've been sleeping there. Since you left."

"Smart move. The bed is the biggest in the place."

"It is. But that's not why."

"Oh." To think she'd thought him so dry, so uncompromising, so stubborn, when he was truly the most warm, wonderful, astonishing man. Again, all she could say was, "Oh."

"Mmm," he said, an enigmatic smile on his face.

Then he leaned against the edge of the doorway, his hands sliding into the front pockets of his jeans. He did that—leaning and wearing jeans—better than anyone she'd ever met. He always seemed so comfortable in his own skin it made her breath hitch. Whereas she often felt as if a colony of flying ants were wriggling under her clothes.

Then he said, "Are you okay? I've been worried about you."

Nobody worried about Little Red Riding Hood. She was the bad ass of the forest. It felt... pretty wonderful. Yet still, old habits died hard, and so she asked, "Whatever for?"

"The way I tore that Band-Aid off, while telling you my concerns about Clancy's motives. As well as the fact I kept it from you at all. In the end I did exactly what my grandmother did to me."

"You were trying to protect me. Just as she was trying to protect you."

Ben nodded, and Nora saw acceptance in his expression. "You are very wise for one so young. Now, want to come in?"

"Yes. Thank you. That would be lovely."

He stood back and waved an arm. She slipped inside, catching his scent as she passed—fresh cotton sheets, woods, and clean male skin. She'd missed it. She'd craved it. She never wanted to go another day without breathing it in.

She had to tell him. But how to tell him when

she'd spent her whole life shoving such emotions deep down inside?

When she turned in the entrance it was to find Ben standing closer than she'd expected. Close enough her nose came level with the second button on his navy Henley T. Close enough to see a day's worth of stubble covering his swarthy jaw. The sparkles of silver therein.

Her gaze felt heavy as she lifted it to his eyes. All those lashes. All that deep lovely brown. It was too much. He was too much. And she loved every bit of him.

She swallowed, squared her shoulders, just a fraction, and said, "I heard what you've chosen to do with the place."

"Oh, you did, did you?"

"You knew Misty would tell me."

He ran a hand up the back of his neck and had the good grace to appear chagrined. "Yeah. I figured that was a safe bet. I know you said I could call on you, ask for your help, but, after you'd been so determined to leave, it didn't feel right to get in your way. So what do you think?"

"I think Clancy would be beyond proud. And this community will be so grateful."

"I asked what *you* think."

Nora's cheeks warmed under his intense gaze. "I think it's perfect, Ben. I think you're—I think you've been more than generous. Which is not a surprise. Because you're—" Nora stopped a moment. Breathed. Pressed her feet into the ground. She could do this. She wanted to do this. "Ben, you're wonderful."

His smile was slow and inviting and addictive. She knew in that moment there wasn't much she wouldn't do to bring out that smile.

"I'm glad you think so," he said. "Didn't feel right, having come all this way, to leave before I'd done what I truly came here to do."

"Sort out the house?"

He shook his head.

"Reconcile with Clancy?"

A smile spread across his face, before his gaze dropped to her mouth. "You do realise I could have done all of that from London, don't you?"

Nora blinked. Well, no. It had not occurred to her. "So then why—?"

His dark gaze lifted till it tangled with hers. "I might not have made it as clear as I thought I had, given that brevity is my preferred style of address, but, Nora, you must know by now that I came here, to this city, to this street, to this house, for you."

Nora felt every good feeling she'd ever felt swelling inside her like a rising current, pushing every sadness, every regret, every fear out of the way. Making just enough room for her to say, "And I waited, here, in this city, in this street, in this house, for you."

Ben breathed out hard. As if *he'd* been sweating *her* response.

As if every woman who ever met him didn't drool, just a little.

As if it weren't patently obvious how taken with him she was.

He went to open his mouth, but she stepped in, lifted onto her toes and pressed a finger to his lips. "I have more to say."

He nodded. Her finger moved with it. As she slid her finger away, his nostrils flared, his eyes dilated. And he waited. She knew in that moment he would wait as long as it took for her to get to where she needed to be. This great, hulking, strong, handsome, generous, measured, patient man, whose forbearance deserved awards.

"I walked away. I walked away because that's what I do. I walk before I'm pushed. Walking *always* feels like a relief. Like I've escaped the jaws of a lion. Walking away from you, though... I didn't like it."

"I should have stopped you."

"You tried."

"Not hard enough. I would have told you, asked you, begged you, held you, kissed you, lassoed you, serenaded you, if I didn't *know* you had to choose to stay, all on your own. And, you know, if I'd had any lassoing skill."

"And if you'd had the rope?" she asked.

"And if I had the rope."

She moved in a little closer.

He noticed. A muscle ticcing in his cheek as if it was taking every ounce of power he had not to do the same.

"I have a question," she said.

Ben's eyes crinkled. All kinds of lights sparkled in their dark depths. "Ask, Nora. Ask me anything you want."

Okay. Here goes. "Is there a chance…? I mean… Do you think that you might ever find it in you to—?"

"Yes."

"Yes?"

"Yes. I love you, Nora. I love you. I'm in love with you. I have been since before I even set foot on the plane to come to you. If missing you so much these past few days I slept in your bed doesn't prove that, then let me tell you again. I love you. Don't get me wrong, you drive me around the bend. But it turns out I really like it there."

Nora stood there, mouth agape, as Ben's words rolled over her in waves of luscious loveliness. And while, in the past, she might have closed down in fear that it couldn't possibly last, she opened herself up to every last drop until she felt as if her bones were made of stardust.

"Nora?" Ben's deep voice came to her like a dream.

She blinked up into his gorgeous gaze and said, "Mmm?"

"Did that answer your question?"

"It did. It really did. Lucky for you, I love you too."

The words fell from her mouth with such ease. And she felt a huge weight lift off her chest. As if a hundred pairs of arms that had been holding her down, holding her back, let go as one.

Ben smiled; with teeth, and crinkling eyes, and all. There was no shock in his expression. No surprise. Just a whole load of relief and a joy that she'd finally realised. That she was finally able to feel it. To own it. To share it with him.

Then, as if he could hold back no longer, Ben moved in, sliding his arms around her and pulling her close. Pulling her flush up against him so that not a sliver of sunshine peeked through.

He pressed a kiss to the top of her head. To the top of her nose. To the edge of her earlobe where his lips stayed as he murmured, "You came out of nowhere, like an invading army from the south, your weapons of choice your determined joy, and passion, and bottomless empathy. I had no clue I'd been living in greyscale till you burst into my life."

Then he placed a kiss on her neck, in that spot that always made her knees give way. And they didn't disappoint. Her breath left her in a sigh that was part groan as shivers rocked through her body.

But he was there to catch her, to hold her, to keep her close.

She pulled away, just enough to reach up and place her hands either side of his face. "If I'm an invading army, then you've made me work for every victory. But it was worth it. You're worth it."

With that, Nora tilted up onto her toes and kissed him. She kissed the man she loved. And she felt it, boy, how she felt it.

In the way he held her, as if she was precious and strong all at once.

In the way he followed her lead in the kiss, while also tempting her to follow his.

In the way he seemed to breathe her in, as if making sure she was real.

When they pulled away, breaths heavy, bodies trembling, Nora leant her head against his chest, then turned so her ear could hear his heart. It was nice to find it sounded as erratic as hers felt. "So what do we do now?"

"I have ideas," said Ben, the tone of his voice enough to send skitters of heat all through her.

"Don't worry, we're both having ideas." Nora grinned against his chest. "I mean, where do we go from here? We are both about to be kicked out of here; sooner rather than later, I'd think, if Misty has any say in the matter."

"Did you know she has a law degree? And an MBA? That before running that wild shop of hers she was a pretty famous civil rights attorney, and she still helps out on pro bono cases?"

Nora closed her eyes and breathed him in. "Sounds about right."

"Mmm…" said Ben, holding her closer.

"Mmm…" said Nora, figuring that if a plane fell on the house she'd die happy. Well, not happy, as she really wanted Ben to follow through with those ideas of his.

"I've been thinking," said Ben.

"You're good at that."

"I really am. So, working remotely has been doable in the short term, but it wouldn't be fair on my team or clients going forward. Meaning I'd have to shut up shop and move it here. Or take a partner. Or sell."

Nora reared back, her gaze dancing between Ben's eyes to see if he was messing with her. He seemed serious. Drop-dead gorgeous, but serious. "What do you mean, *sell*? You can't sell the Desk of Bennett J Hawthorne. It's where I found you. It's a part of you! It's where you earned your cape. And what about Damon and the team? They've come so far."

Ben laughed. "Trust you to think of everyone before yourself."

Nora's nose wrinkled. "Nah. I mean, yes, but I'm mostly thinking of you. *And* me. I took a holiday to Bali a few years ago. Do you think my passport might still be valid? Do I need a visa to go to London?"

"What about your island?"

"My—the *resort*? Are you suggesting you'd move your company to a beach hut on the Great Barrier Reef? For me?"

"I'd move to the moon if it meant I got to wake up to this face every day."

She kissed him again. A kiss that made her see stars.

Before she completely went under his spell, she dragged herself back. "That gig, it's not for me. I'd be spending my days alone, writing puff pieces for some rich dudes. I prefer making a pittance working for people I can look in the eye. People who appreciate it. People who actually need *me*. *The Girl Upstairs* can create content anywhere. And if you're so het up on living on an island, England is an island, right?"

"Again," he said, his thumb tracing the edge of her nose. "So wise. So very wise. Now, are we done with all the talking? Because I'm still having those ideas I mentioned earlier. Ideas that involve getting you naked and horizontal and, since we could be kicked out at any moment, I think it best we get cracking—"

Nora leapt at him then, throwing her arms around his neck. And he caught her, as he always had. Kissing her, and carrying her slowly, carefully, deliberately, up the stairs.

Because they really were precarious for a man with such big feet.

* * * * *

*If you enjoyed this story, check out
these other great reads from Ally Blake*

Dream Vacation, Surprise Baby
Brooding Rebel to Baby Daddy
Crazy About Her Impossible Boss
A Week with the Best Man

All available now!